IVY LITVINOV was born in London in 1889. Her father, Walter Low, a late-Victorian progressive, died when she was five years old and her mother, Alice Baker, remarried in 1896. Ivy attended Maida Vale High School and then, in 1905, contributed the first of many articles to the *Manchester Guardian*. Whilst working at the Prudential, her first novel, *Growing Pains* (1913), appeared, swiftly followed by *The Questing Beast* (1914). Both are strongly autobiographical. By this time she had various literary friends including Viola Meynell, Catherine Carswell and D.H. Lawrence.

A few weeks after the outbreak of War, she met the influential Bolshevik revolutionary, Maxim Litvinov, who was in close collaboration with Lenin. The couple married in 1916 and had two children. With the onset of the Revolution, Maxim returned to Russia and the family joined him in Moscow two years later. There Ivy Litvinov became a respected translator, an English teacher, and wrote *His Master's Voice* (1930). Meanwhile, Maxim had become an international diplomat, admired in the West for his commitment to disarmament. After a brief fall from grace (1939-41), fortunes turned when Maxim was appointed ambassador to Washington; but in 1945 he again fell victim to a Stalinist purge. They returned to Moscow where Maxim died six years later; his last words were for Ivy, 'Englishwoman, go home.'

She did not take up his challenge for some years but remained in Moscow as a translator and also worked on, but did not complete, the hybrid of fiction and autobiography she called 'Sorterbiography'.

Ivy Litvinov visited England briefly in 1960 and returned for good in 1972. She settled in Hove where her daughter Tanya joined her four years later. She continued to write into her eighth decade: several of her stories were published in *The New Yorker* before being collected in *She Knew She Was Right* (1971; Virago 1988).

Ivy Litvinov died in 1977.

D0266937

HIS MASTER'S VOICE

A Detective Story

IVY LITVINOV

VIRAGO

Published by VIRAGO PRESS Limited 1989
20-23 Mandela Street, London NW1 0HQ

First published 1930
by William Heinemann Ltd
under the author's maiden name Ivy Low
Copyright Ivy Low 1930
Revised edition © Ivy Litvinov 1973

British Library Cataloguing in Publication Data

Litvinov, Ivy, 1889-1977
   His master's voice
   I. Title
   823'.912[F]

   ISBN 0-86068-104-1

Printed in Great Britain by
Cox & Wyman Ltd, Reading, Berkshire

To
VEROCHKA

CONTENTS

TO THE READER

His Master's Voice opens on a bitter night in February, 1926, beneath the wall of the Kremlin; it ends before the ballet season closes for the summer. February nights are still bitter cold in Moscow, the Kremlin wall still stands, and the ballet season runs from September to June. Almost everything else has changed. "White-Walled Moscow", the legendary city of holy muddle, will never come back.

The Kremlin itself—a glorious mixture of styles, to which each period, from the Tatar invasion to the present day, has made its contribution—still rises behind its ancient walls, looking more than ever as if intended for some other race, remote and long extinct. There is still a sprinkle of private mansions, monuments to the fantasy of the Moscow merchant in the late nineties ... decked out with battlements and mullioned windows ... with perfectly useless balconies plastered along their fronts, in which a man of full habit could hardly have stood. They belong to the period once known as "art-nouveau", and still called "moderne" in Moscow, and they bear unmistakable signs of having gone up during the aesthetic revival of 1905, when wardrobes had lyre-shaped cutouts in their pediments, and walls and ash trays were adorned with pre-Raphaelite damsels in high relief, on a background of spaghetti and lily pads.

The witches' cauldrons, where homeless children dozed all night against the cooling sides of great vats of tar, have gone from the streets, and gone are the children who sought their warmth.

The buildings which have changed the streets of Moscow have changed the lives of the people in her streets. Their operation brought to the city a new population—office workers to staff the new government departments, bus drivers to drive the new motorbuses, teachers for the new schools, students from all over the Union for the new colleges.

Fifty years ago it was normal for a night watchman and his entire family to inhabit one room in an old house, and for the night watchman's wife to get up in the morning to make her lodger's tea on a primus stove in the same room. Now it would be normal for them to have a flat in a tall house on the site of the crumbling two-storey mansion they inhabit in *His Master's Voice*. And they would not have the baby in bed with them; the mother would have learned, on her visits to the local Infant Welfare Centre, that babies must sleep alone. The bachelor lodger would have his own flat. Tamara, the ballet-girl heroine, would no longer live in the workshop of her shoemaker uncle amid the high stench of leather. The wicked still flee when no man pursueth, but the absconding dentist would have been held up by traffic lights, he would really have flown, and the police would have had airports to watch as well as railway stations.

I should not be surprised to discover that the manicurist still receives clients in her room, for she is one of those women who do not change.

All the people who were young in *His Master's Voice* would have grown up into a new world, but none of them have changed so much as Moscow's street children. The little wolves of society, who play such an important part in this book, became the objects of a supreme salvage campaign, drawing them from the streets into the training centres, and returning them, as new citizens, to society. During the years of training they may have become engineers, truck drivers, scientists, and musicians. If a congress, a change of job, or a vacation, brought them back to Moscow after an absence of ten years, they would not know the streets which once harboured them. They would search in vain for the sprawling markets, cluttering the cramped pavements with the bodies and wares of vendors of hot pies, shoelaces, "butter-brodi" and brassières, and making it easy for an active boy to lift a fountain pen from a breast pocket, snatch a purse, clutch at a fistful of bills from an incautiously opened handbag, or even slash a panel from the back of a coat.

Readers have changed too since His Master's Voice *came out in London. William Heinemann, the English publisher, who also brought out my first novel, written in the first decade of the century, and the second of my life, advised me to stick to my maiden name (Ivy Low), as "readers of detective fiction prefer an*

English author". The book could not then be placed in the United States at all, publishers' readers reporting "too much Russian background ... readers of mystery stories don't want a lot of atmosphere ... we advise Ivy Low to cut out the stuff about spring over the Kremlin, and put in another murder or two".

Today the Russian background and the stuff about spring over the Kremlin are likely to be the most interesting features of the book.

One other person is separated by almost half a century from the time this book was first published—the author. I feel no surprise to have seen so much happen in so short a time. And yet I think the image of myself which I find in these pages is still valid. The things that interested me then interest me now. Little girls still play hopscotch on the pavements, the ice is still borne through the town on the breast of the river in the spring. I took no camera, I made no notes, but the pictures have remained. I have lived through fifty years of "live" history—years in which eager travellers came for a week, a month, a year, returning to their own countries to write about education, art, politics—and all I have to show is a mystery story about a ballet girl.

HIS MASTER'S VOICE

CHAPTER I

WHAT THE MOON SAW

THE TOWN SEEMED not so much asleep as strangled, locked in frost. The Kremlin palace and its numerous churches and spires looked down over toothed walls on silent squares, empty bridges, and abandoned streets. On summer evenings it looks down on its own reflection in the water, regally quiescent; on this bitter night in February, 1926, when the frozen river refused to mirror its crude walls and fantastic buildings, it was more like a picture in a book for children than anything that had ever answered to the requirements of human beings. The great wall turns a proud flank upon the sprawl of the Red Square, as if ignoring the line of shamelessly ugly buildings, raised in the unaesthetic eighties to spoil one of the most perfect squares that a town ever had, and simply turns its back upon the boulevard flanking it at the west, where what was once a moat has exchanged the function of keeping the vulgar away from the sacred walls for that of harbouring the masses in their moments of relaxation. Here at least, even on this ice-bound night, is life of a sort, for every bare branch of the trees planted at regular intervals each side of the gravelled walks, alternately with seats and spittoons, bears its winter fruit—sleeping ravens, huddled densely on the bough, and looking at a little distance like last year's leaves still clinging to the trees.

At every street corner stood two or three droshkies, the drivers huddled up in their quilted coats, tied in the middle with faded red sashes, dozing on their seats, heads sunk on breasts, arms folded. The horses, poor beasts, seemed to be rapt into a sort of trance of cold, their eyelashes, and the short soft hairs in their nostrils and over their velvety nozzles, frozen into needle-like spikes. At the gateway of every yard and on the doorstep of every shop, drowsed the night watchmen, swathed in long sheepskin coats and looking rather like Robinson Crusoes in their high, shaggy caps.

The night watchman before a gate in one of the small streets running west of the Kremlin wall and almost in the shadow, felt numb to the spine. The great clock in the Spassky Tower boomed out midnight, and as its vibrations died on the still cold air the watchman realised that he had not seen a single soul since he had taken up his post at eight o'clock that evening. No one had come in or out of the yard, no one had passed in the silent street. The long stillness and death-like silences were ordeals to which the nerves of the gnarled old man were still susceptible. On tender spring evenings his vigil was not so arduous, for then the young people lingered arm-in-arm up and down the quiet street half the night, music and bursts of laughter escaped from the open windows, and the people in the houses came and went through the gate at all hours, exchanging friendly salutations with its guardian; the breeze rustled sweetly in the lilac bushes, and their sweet scent did not abhor the wide and hairy recesses of the watchman's nostrils, while his ears were often gladdened by the clip-clop of the droshky horses as they trotted merrily past, bearing a couple of young men in blouses and high boots, absorbed in earnest discussion, or an enlaced and silent pair, rapt in contemplation of each other's faces. Even an occasional drunk, staggering past and mildly remonstrating with an imaginary opponent, or singing raucously, helped to relieve the tedium and shoulder the long hours along, but now not even a stray cat or homeless dog came in the black, silent frost to vary the monotony and people the solitude. Only the empty, snowy street and the cold, brilliant stars returned the old man's wistful gaze with a hard and icy stare.

He dozed and woke the long hours through until the paling sky told him that his tedious vigil had come to an end, and that he could now turn in for a sleep in bed. He rose stiffly from the step, rubbing his frozen hands together and stamping on the snow. He was not a tall man, but the long coat made him look almost gigantic. Stepping clumsily through its folds over the lintel, he craned his neck to catch sight of the clock tower. It was still too dark for his old eyes to see the dial, but just then the air shook with the stroke of six. Yes, the night watchman was free and could go home to bed. He shambled, bear-like, across the slippery snow to the two-storey house in the middle of the yard, stopping at the low porch which protected a padded, leather-covered door.

From deep folds in the sheepskin coat he produced a mammoth key, and the door creaked and swung before him. In the pitchy dark within he turned to a low door at the right, which he unlocked with another key, no poor relation of the first, and stumbled over his coat into the passage. After the frosty yard the air here seemed close and warm, though the actual temperature was probably not many degrees higher, but when, having divested himself of his coat and cap, he entered the room in which his entire family was sleeping, he encountered a stench which would have knocked down anybody but a Moscow night watchman. Stepanovich, however, recognised it gratefully, thankful to have escaped from the biting cold. With stiff, jerky movements he took off his jacket and trousers, gave himself a good scratch all over, and rolled into bed in his rough grey singlet.

Now the Stepanovich family was complete and united—father, mother, and a miscellany of children, from the eldest daughter of sixteen, to the baby in the washing basket across two chairs beside the bed. No ray of light hinted that dawn was already spreading over the town, not a breath of air suggested that thirty degrees of frost were registered on the thermometer outside the window. The old man fell heavily asleep almost immediately, his mouth open and his nose emitting stertorous snores, but his bedmate, the grey old woman whose shrivelled body had but recently borne him a sound and healthy baby-girl, disturbed by his entry, moaned now and again and turned restlessly from side to side. But for these movements and the occasional sound of scratching deep silence reigned in the room for another two hours.

The old woman—she may have been about 45, but she had long been grey and almost toothless—woke up just as the clock was striking eight. It was a Sunday, and none of the children had to go to school, so she had nobody to rouse. She slid out of bed and began groping about the floor for certain indescribably shapeless and colourless garments. The baby in the basket stirred and whimpered, puckering up its tiny face and turning its head from side to side on the soiled and soured pillow. She bent over the basket and picked up the damp and smelling infant, which, despite its unhygienic condition looked the picture of placid health. She unbuttoned her dress and her hand went searching for the long, shrivelled breast, at which the baby sucked eagerly—

a hag, a witch, with warm, sweet milk surging through her veins.
After allowing the baby to suck vigorously for twenty minutes,
she put it into the bed beside its father, and shuffled across the
room. Her pumping of the primus stove aroused nobody in the
room, and by the time the kettle was boiling she had a tray
neatly fixed up with glass, plate, knife, pat of butter, a couple
of rolls and a small teapot, with which she padded into the passage
and up a staircase, towards a door at the top, under which she
was surprised to see a line of light. If Arkady Petrovich Pavlov
could have seen the room from which his neat tray emerged
every morning, his enjoyment of his early morning tea and bread
and butter might have been slightly marred. But he was not to
enjoy tea and bread and butter this morning, for when the watchman's wife opened the door she dropped the tray with a crash,
spilling the hot tea, and breaking the glass into smithereens.
And he was never to enjoy anything in this world again. It was
the sight of his dead body seated at the table in the full glare
of an electric lamp hanging from the ceiling, with a dark stream
of blood running from his chair almost to the door that had
made the affrighted woman drop tray, teapot and all, and stand
transfixed with horror on the threshold, unable to take her gaze
from the dreadful sight.

At first she had been so terrified that she could neither move
nor utter a sound, but the next moment she emitted a scream
so piercing that it seemed as if even the figure at the table must
have heard it. But it remained dreadfully still, the head dropped
forward on to a square black box on the table with the hinged lid
just resting on his hair. She noticed then that a dagger was sticking out of the side of his neck, and that it was from this point
that the blood was flowing. After letting out another scream or
two she turned and fled, leaving the tray and its contents scattered
about the passage.

The silence and darkness of her own familiar room, the heavy
peaceful breathing of her husband and children, almost made her
feel for the fraction of a second that what she had seen upstairs
must have been a nightmare from which she would shortly
awake. But then its *reality* forced itself upon her, in a way reality
has, even in retrospect, and she seized her husband by the shoulder.
It was difficult to rouse the sleeping bear, he only growled, rolled
over and took the baby in his arms. But the woman persevered

until he opened eyes set like jewels in the creased mahogany of his cheeks. At the same time a boy raised a tousled head from his pillow and stared about him in the gloom. The woman hurried across to the window and began pulling at the shutters.

Even when the whole family was awake she could not at first penetrate the drowsy brain of her husband, but the two boys, Mitya and Sanya, were soon on the floor, barefoot and eager, crowding round their mother, and a girl of about fourteen was firing out shrill questions from her bed on a low wooden frame on the floor. In less than no time the boys had on their trousers and felt boots and, snatching up their short, padded jackets and leather storm-caps, had darted across the snowy yard to the Chief of the Porters.

The Chief of the Porters used to be a very great man indeed in Russian houses. His acquaintance was sought and rewarded by wood-merchants, and menders of stoves, plumbers, and other craftsmen, for the householder in distress always turned first to the Porter, and his recommendation was powerful. He has come down in the world nowadays, for although lists of all residents still have to be made and houses kept in repair, this work is now done by the House Committee, and the porter only carries out its instructions.

When you are given the number of a street in Moscow, you go there, if you are a foreigner and inexperienced, in the confident expectation of finding the house you want. But really your troubles are only just beginning, for the number is quite as likely as not to stand for a kind of landed estate, possibly including huge blocks of flats, four or five two-storey cottages and a couple of sheds which may or may not be inhabited. This was very much the case in the yard guarded by Stepanovich from eight in the evening till six o'clock in the morning. Over the top of the gate was painted the number 49, but when you had stepped over the lintel you would be hard put to it to know where to turn to find the flat you wanted. The house inhabited by the night watchman and the murdered Pavlov was a two-storied stucco affair, decked out with absurd battlements and mullioned windows, and it had several perfectly useless little balconies plastered along its fronts, balconies in which a man of a full habit could hardly have stood—a characteristic example of the fantasy of the Moscow merchant in the later nineties and first decade of the present century, the merchant who had made good and intended to build his own pet idea of what a house should be, and to keep the architect well in hand. Such houses, usually more remarkable than beautiful, are seldom comfortable and never convenient. The ornate squatness of this one looked still more absurd by reason of its being hemmed in by a towering mass of modern red brick flats on either side. The Chief of the Porters, whose province was the whole estate, inhabited a room in a semi-basement flat in one of these buildings.

At first the old man was inclined to disbelieve the incoherent story poured out by Sanya and Mitya, knowing them well for a pair of monkeying lads, ever ready to play a joke on an old man come down in the world. Ah, time was when Simyon Simyonvich had been a respected and loved member of the family in the grand little turreted mansion in the middle of the yard, long before there was ever a six-storey building in Moscow, and little boys very different from Sanya and Mitya had come to him for a whistle or a carved walking-stick—little boys with rosy cheeks and neat suits, and curls lovingly arranged over their foreheads. One didn't see such little boys among the crop-headed Moscow ragamuffins. When, however, the dull brain had at last realised that murder had been committed and death was sitting in the house, he put down the rag with which he had been polishing the door-handle, shouldered on his discoloured, wadded jacket, and followed the excited boys out into the yard. Instead of going straight to the house, however, he went into the street, always followed by Mitya and Sanya, and made his way to the militia-man at the corner, who, after a few words from the porter, followed him back to the house. For the Chief of the Porters knew his duty, if others didn't, and he knew very well that if murder or any other crime had been committed, you couldn't have the police on the spot too soon. Closely followed by the awestruck boys, the old porter and the young militia-man passed in the footsteps of the night watchman from the street gate to the porch of the little mansion. There the old man suddenly turned and dismissed Mitya and Sanya savagely. The watchman, already dressed, though considerably docked of his lawful allowance of sleep, was standing at his door, the baby in his arms. He went in and shut the door as the militia-man and porter appeared, as if he felt that his curiosity might be regarded as indecent. The two men stumped up the stairs till they reached the door at the top, that door on the threshold of which the night watchman's wife had dropped her tray in her horror and fled. It was ajar, as she had left it, with the debris of the glass on the floor, gleaming in the electric light. The younger man went straight into the room, the old man standing aghast at the door, unable for a moment to move his old limbs. He had known the dead man personally, and that made his death much more dreadful. The militia-man, after a quick look round the room, made his way to the telephone, and rang up the district headquarters of the militia. He touched nothing in the room, but pushed the old man away from the door, kicked a few shards of glass from the threshold that prevented the closing of the door, which he then shut, taking up his post outside with an air of immense importance. A young, fair man, with pale blue eyes under the peak of his red and blue cap, looking sturdier than he really was, in his full, belted coat of blue navy cloth. He spent the interval before the powers that he had summoned by telephone appeared, in shooing away the children who kept appearing on the staircase, and frowning at some women who stood at the bottom of the stairs, peeping up with a fearful joy in their eyes.

CHAPTER II

"...IT WASN'T YOU..."

DISTRICT PROCURATOR NIKULIN was not pleased to be called by telephone at 9.30 on a Sunday morning. He considered it his full and perfect right to sleep till half past ten on a Sunday morning, and to linger over the day's paper and his coffee until lunch time.

"And yet," he said to himself, "how seldom am I able to realise this modest ideal. There is something positively perverse in the way in which crimes are committed in Moscow on a Saturday night. I believe they do it out of sheer malice."

He gazed with antipathy at his morning face in the glass, inspected his chin closely to see if he really must absolutely shave, and decided there was no real must or absolute about it, took his daily glance with a hand-glass at the tonsure that was beginning to dawn through the thin hair at the top of his head, to see if it had grown overnight. Decided gloomily that it had. He had scarcely finished his not very elaborate toilet when a ring was heard in the passage. The woman who did for Nikulin daily, answered the door and the Investigator himself opened the door of his room and popped his head into the passage.

"That you, Yanovitsky?" he cried. "Come on in and sit down. I shan't be a moment."

Detective Yanovitsky, after a short time spent at the coat-stand in the passage, entered the room on stamping feet. This detective was a distinctly low-brow character, having nothing in common with the suave gentlemen in English and American detective stories, who speak like undergraduates and think nothing of following up a clue in Montmartre or Mexico. It is highly probable that Detective Yanovitsky's principal qualifications were a wide knowledge of crime gained by first-hand experience and an extensive acquaintance among the brotherhood that makes crime a profession. Be this as it may, he had a ruffianly physiognomy and short blunt fingers, with the thumbs turned well back. And whenever his Chief addressed him he drew himself up, his thumbs to his trouser seams and seemed always just to be on the point of saluting. Most of his replies to questions were in the nature of "Yessir!" Nossir!" or their present-day Russian equivalent. Literally he said: "Precisely, Citizen Procurator!" "I hear and obey, Citizen Procurator!" And withal the rogue had a human gleam in his small, wicked eyes, and a grin that was really likeable.

"Why is all the murdering in Moscow done on Saturday nights, Yanovitsky? Can you tell me that?" asked Nikulin, tying up his bootlaces and looking up at the detective from over his knee.

"Yes, Citizen Procurator," was the prompt reply.

"No, really! Can you?" said the Procurator. "Then tell me, if you think you know."

"Yes, Citizen Procurator. End of the week, Citizen Procurator. More inclination for relaxation on eve of day of rest, Citizen Procurator."

The Procurator regarded him with interest.

"I thought a murderer looked on a little killing as part of the day's work," he said. "I didn't know you and your friends considered it in the light of relaxation."

Since Yanovitsky had never actually been convicted of killing anyone he supposed he was justified in regarding his Chief's insinuation as a pleasantry, and therefore duly permitted his enormous black moustache-ends to twitch themselves upright and leave a set of sound white teeth exposed in a respectful grin as he replied:

"No, Citizen Procurator! Not the murderers. Those who are murdered. Gentlemen are usually murdered during relaxation, Citizen Procurator."

"I believe you're right," replied Nikulin thoughtfully. "You ought to know if any one does."

He stared at the detective meditatively, wondering how much there was in his theory and if relaxation included or signified in Yanovitsky's vocabulary being drunk.

"Suppose you go down and hunt around for a droshky," he said.

"The District Station has already sent a car," said Yanovitsky, coming to attention again.

"Has it? Then you can go down and sit in it. I shall be with you in a couple of minutes."

Hastily swallowing his coffee and milk and a thickly buttered roll, the Procurator collected some writing material, packed what he required in his briefcase and slammed the door on his bachelor establishment. He was a tall, loosely-built man of forty-five, looking rather older, perhaps owing to carelessness of clothing, perhaps to carelessness of diet and lack of suitable exercise. For the rest he had a kindly, weary eye lighting up his rather large and rather flabby face.

He found Yanovitsky standing on the pavement beside a worn but handsome limousine. Two young men in khaki, also standing about on the snowy pavement, jumped into the seat for one beside the chauffeur, as soon as the District Procurator, followed by Detective Yanovitsky, had entered the car.

On their arrival at the two-storey house in the yard the young policeman at the door of the death chamber was released from his post and sent back to resume—with evident reluctance—his monotonous vigil at the corner of the street where nothing ever happened.

Leaving his khaki-clad escort posted at the top and bottom of the stairs, with strict injunctions to allow nobody past them but the doctor, the Procurator, followed by the detective, entered the room. For a few moments they stood at the door, making a general survey. It was a small, squarish room, comfortably, almost richly furnished. In the middle stood a square table, covered with a white cloth, and obviously made ready for supper for two. The dead man was seated with his head resting on a black box, of which the hinged, open lid almost hid his face. The handle of a dagger, sticking out of his neck like the key of an automatic toy, caught the light from a hanging lamp. A strap in the other side of the box showed it to be a portable gramophone. Next to the door stood a bureau writing-table with the flap let down, exposing letters, papers and journals in some confusion. The corner of the room was cut off by a Dutch stove with gleaming white tiles. A door at right angles to the room evidently led into the bedroom. Two club armchairs and a deep divan, all in leather, and with no cushions beyond their own upholstering, were grouped on the far side of the table, near to these stood a well-appointed smoker's table, bearing a silver cigarette-box;

a couple of good rugs lay on the polished parquet floor and a glass-paned bookcase and four insipid oil-paintings (two still-lifes and a couple of smiling heads) made up the principal inventory of the room, as far as the eye could take in at a first cursory look round. The second survey led to amplifications and fresh discoveries: a china figurine of a dancing girl, pretty obviously belonging to the category of "Paris goods" and very up to date at that, in a mauve chemise of real crêpe-de-chine and real silk stockings, and rouging her lips with a real lipstick, was posed on the top of the writing table. Next to her, not very appropriately, stood a large unframed photograph, mounted on grey embossed cardboard, showing a goods train at a country station, loaded with freshly-cut timber, a group of stolid-looking men in linen blouses, under which was written in Russian: "Opening of the OBLESS, Lomsk, Spring, 1925."

While the Procurator was making his notes a slight stir was heard in the passage, and the door opened to admit the doctor. Dr. Popov was one of those Russians never to be seen without a week's growth of beard on their chins, but eternally protesting that they had had no time to shave yesterday. The three men shook hands and the doctor went straight over to the body. While he was examining it, one of the men outside put his head into the room to say that the van had arrived from the mortuary, and at the Procurator's word of permission, two white-clad men were admitted, carrying between them a stretcher.

"Before he's taken away I should like to have that dagger," said the Procurator, drawing near to the table.

"Well, wait a moment, supposing we straighten him up first," said the doctor. "Come here, you fellows, and give us a hand."

The white-clad men went up to the body, one on each side, and took it under the armpits, preparatory to raising it. The absorbed instinctive silence was suddenly broken by a raucous, snarling sound. The men holding up the body almost lost their grip and the other three started violently. Then the room was filled with a strong, tender voice.

"By God, Chaliapin!" exclaimed the Procurator.

The dead man was propped against the back of the chair, his head dropping on his chest, the dagger sticking out. The disc revolved to its end, the deep, bass notes interrupted at every cycle by a raucous snarl as the needle came up against the zig-zag crack caused by the weight of the dead man's head. Only when the needle came to the centre of the disc did the Procurator, mopping his forehead, step forward and lift up the sound-box. The disc went on revolving with a soft whirr for a few seconds, and then stopped of itself. The men in the room seemed ashamed to meet each other's eyes. Something queer had happened, something ghastly, they felt. And yet all that had actually happened was that a weight had been removed from a gramophone wound up to full tension. But everybody felt that a ghostly stranger had entered among them, raised his voice, and gone. And they all felt that they had been in some way caught unawares by the voice of the stranger.

The Procurator was the first to recover.

"I think we might let in a little daylight now," he said, and Yanovitsky went eagerly to the window to draw back the thick curtains, while somebody near the door switched off the electricity.

Before leaving the house the Procurator interviewed both Stepanovich, the night watchman, and the old man Volkov, the head porter. The former he found to be a bear-like soul, inarticulate, rather than uncommunicative, who seemed incapable of giving a clear account of the night through which he had just passed. He was, however, evidently trying to answer in good faith all the questions put to him, making obvious efforts to be extremely precise in his replies, and the Procurator soon felt himself to be in possession of what was probably a full and authentic account of events which took place in the yard and before the gate, between twelve o'clock midnight and two o'clock in the morning. Soon after twelve his ears had been cheered by the sound of a Fan automobile a street away. He could hear it long before he saw it, and he saw the slanting panels of light from its lamps before he could make out its dark body. It drew up with a grinding of brakes right at his feet, and as soon as it stopped the door opened and a woman alighted and stood under the lamp in the snow, while a man, who had followed her out of the taxi, paid the driver. When the man turned towards the gate the night watchman recognised him immediately as Arkady Petrovich Pavlov, who rented a couple of rooms in the house in the middle of the yard. Pavlov had wished him good evening and remarked that it was a cold night. Arkady Petrovich always had a kind word for everybody. And the young lady—she looked young and shy—had also said good evening very prettily. The watchman had been sorry when they had gone, and sorry that, as Arkady Petrovich had the key to his door in the side of the house there was no need for him to accompany them. He would have welcomed the diversion of a few extra seconds of human companionship. He reminded himself that he must not forget, when the lady had gone, to go and see that Pavlov's door was locked. Arkady Petrovich hardly ever remembered to lock it, and when reminded, would always frown and say he must absolutely see about getting an American lock, which would lock automatically. But he never did see about it, and the night watchman was comfortably sure he never would. After all, what did it matter? So long as old Stepanovich stood at the gate no harm was likely to happen to anybody in the house.

When the taxi had buzzed away the night had seemed emptier than ever. The night watchman even thought it seemed colder. Then he dozed on his canvas stool. Perhaps he really went off for a moment or two, anyhow it seemed only a short time after this that the young lady was passing him again, stepping through a small door cut in the big green gate, and wishing him goodnight with the utmost friendliness. He watched the compact figure walk briskly away from him down the street, and presently he heard the Kremlin clock strike the hour—four quarters and a single stroke. Only one o'clock. He was just thinking to himself that the young lady hadn't stopped as long as what Arkady Petrovich's guests usually did, when those blamed boys got the better of him again, just when he was telling himself that he must go and see if Arkady Petrovich had locked the door after his guest. Two of them it was and they seemed, as usual, to appear out of nowhere, ducking under his arm through the gate, and disappearing into the yard. Stepanovich had waddled helplessly after them, as he always did, looking conscientiously into the woodshed and behind the sandbin, seeking for any place in which street boys might conceivably be supposed to take shelter from the cold. But to-night, as on all other nights, he had failed to discover their hiding place, and he knew that to-night, as on all other nights, he would not see them return. He could only suppose that they had some hidy-hole on the back staircase of the tall flats that backed upon the yard—*his* yard—but were no business of his, since their front gave on to the street on the other side, parallel to that on which the gate guarded by Stepanovich opened. Notwithstanding this, however, to-night, as every night, he waddled over to the flats, poking about the dark stairs and growling in his beard, but finding no trace of the boys. After a few minutes of fruitless search, he had padded back to his gate, and his short naps were disturbed no more that night, except by the cold, and the striking of the hours, which always waked him.

The old man was surprised at being questioned as to the identity of the young woman who had left the house shortly before one, with her whom he had seen go in with Pavlov, soon after midnight. It had evidently not occurred to him for a moment to doubt that they were one and the same, but under cross-examination his conscience, or perhaps it was his native caution, would not allow him to make a definite statement, and he would only repeat again and again that he hadn't taken that much notice, and so really couldn't say. Maybe it was the same young lady both times, but again maybe it was different young ladies, he couldn't say for sure, for he hadn't taken that much notice. The Procurator, however, felt pretty sure that little doubt existed in the man's mind. Himself he felt no doubt at all. She who had left before one was the same she who had arrived, with Pavlov, after twelve, and highly likely to prove to be she who had murdered him with a small, but mortally sharp, Caucasian dagger.

The head porter, having been indoors and in bed all night, had little of value to report, but, perhaps for that very reason, was the more inclined to be garrulous. He had said to Stepanovich that very evening, on passing by him at the gate, that it was a lonesome job for a man to be standing all night in the street and he had ought to be careful, with these here roughs knocking about the streets at night, a man of his age, he had indeed, and he wouldn't care to do it himself, for all he had been a matter of forty years in that very yard, and knew every nook and corner of it like the palm of his own hand, but still the place for a man going on in years was his bed at night, and there's no going against that. And a kinder, more open-hearted sort of gentleman than Arkady Petrovich he never wished to see, and there weren't many like him left now, more's the pity. And more in this strain, till the Procurator, having got all the information Volkov could furnish, was forced to dam the torrent of speech by sending him away with a courteous word of thanks, that was far from mollifying the snubbed old man, who went off muttering in his beard.

After noting down that Arkady Petrovich Pavlov, Moscow representative of the Obless timber firm, had been found dead, with a Caucasian dagger in his neck at 9 a.m. on Sunday, February 14th, and filling in all the necessary details, the Procurator left the scene of the murder and went home to dinner.

CHAPTER III

"...IT WASN'T YOU..."

A FEW HOURS later the Procurator sat in his office surveying his spoils. On the table before him lay the dagger, returned for dactylographical and microscopic examination, its bright blade rusted with blood. It was a Caucasian instrument of a kind easily recognisable by any Russian; the long blade was sharpened on both sides right up to the hilt, the point sharp and slender, and the handle was elaborately chased and inlaid. A thing of cruel beauty, and undoubtedly the most important piece of accusatory evidence. Beside it lay two coins of gilded tinfoil, with holes pierced in them—the sort of thing that fancy-dress gipsies wear on their fancy-dress boleros. And next came a programme for the Bolshoi Theatre, bearing the date of the day before. In a corner stood the black box of the gramophone, the record on which Pavlov had been murdered still on it.

By now the Procurator had had time to go through the dead man's papers and had established that he was the manager of the Moscow branch of the Obless, a Siberian timber concession in the hands of an American firm. He had discovered also that the late Mr. Pavlov had had a great admiration for the ballet, or at least for the members of the corps de ballet, for he had taken the trouble to cut out of journals—mostly French and German—the photograph of many a smiling damsel or bevy of beauties in gauze skirts and flesh tights, and had also—to judge by the number of French journals he had kept in a drawer in his desk—been a great admirer of light Parisian literature. Very few private letters had been kept, and all those that were there bore foreign addresses, and would probably be easy to follow up—two from a sister in New York, one from a friend in London, asking for influence in obtaining a Russian visa. There was only one with no name and address, and this was evidently not a letter, but a note which seemed to have been written in the dead man's room and on his own paper. 'Sorry not to have found you.

Waited three quarters of an hour. Your old hag said you would be in any minute, but you didn't come. Have to be at the theatre by 7.30 so must go." This note was simply signed "S" and had probably been kept by accident, having been written on the top page of the writing pad and not torn off.

While the Procurator was studying these details the detective Yanovitsky looked in to report. He had interviewed the family of the night watchman and the head porter, and seemed very angry at having found out nothing against any of them. The Procurator, who, after having interviewed Stepanovich and Volkov felt pretty sure that neither of them had had anything to do with the murder, had not pressed his investigations in this quarter very close, but had sent the detective to find out all he could about the neighbourhood. Of course there was nothing actually to preclude the possibility of either the night watchman or the porter having been the murderers, or accomplices of the murderer, but it seemed to the Procurator highly improbable. Such people are usually tried and proven servants, and their only likely motive for murder could have been theft which, supposing them to have been dishonest they could probably have committed often enough in the given case without resorting to murder. Lastly the dagger used was a Caucasian dagger, and the only knife either the porter or the night watchman could possibly have been supposed to possess, if they possessed a knife at all, would be the much shorter Finnish knife, lovingly called the "Finnka". Of course it was not impossible that the dead man had been murdered with a dagger of his own, kept as an objet d'art, but then the Procurator would have expected to find the scabbard somewhere, for there would have been no point in a murderer carrying off such a dangerous piece of evidence against himself. Most conclusive of all—Pavlov had been killed by a thrust in the jugular, practically the only place in which a man could be instantaneously killed by a dagger, and it would be extravagant to expect a slow-moving, slow-thinking bear of a man like Stepanovich, or a stiff old porter like Volkov, to know that. And now the detective had brought finger-prints of the whole family and none of them coincided with the two prints found on the hilt of the dagger, although those of the watchman's wife were much in evidence on plates and glasses and on the side of the door—as might have been expected, considering that she "did" his room.

Yanovitsky had, however, more to tell. He had established the fact that there were no other residents in the house except the night watchman and the late Pavlov, who had occupied two rooms on the first floor. The ground floor and the attics were kept boarded up, and showed no signs of having been tampered with, though a fairly heavy fall of snow at about seven o'clock, when a sudden rise in the temperature was observed, would, of course, have obliterated all footsteps. Yanovitsky had also traced the night cabbies to their lair, and had found one who had seen a lady just by the Church of St. Basil the Blessed, on the Red Square, just as the clock was striking a quarter past one, had offered to drive her home and had been refused.

Thus a most important fact was firmly established at the outset and the night watchman's halting tale confirmed: a woman had been with Pavlov between twelve and one. The Procurator already had the doctor's statement that the murder must have taken place between twelve and two.

While Yanovitsky had been pursuing his investigations the usual crowd of spectators had collected around the house, mostly poorly-dressed men and women with shawls over their heads, but there had been one lady in a grand fur coat, who had gazed up at the window, and kept on questioning the watchman's wife with tearful interest, indeed twice she had to wipe tears from her eyes. The detective had made inquiries and discovered that she inhabited a flat in the big block on the other side of the yard. Conversation with Volkov elicited the information that she was a manicurist by profession, but was suspected of having gentlemen friends who contributed to her welfare.

The Procurator looked at his finger nails. They certainly warranted a visit to a manicurist, but were a little short for her to be able to do anything with them. However, he thought it would not be a bad idea to make acquaintance with this lady in a way so as not to alarm her or rouse her suspicions. He therefore made his way to the house he had already visited to-day, not without a preliminary selection of a particular tie that he kept for more festive occasions, and a good smoothing down of his hair at the parting with sweet-smelling oil. He regretted that he had no scent for his handkerchief; it seemed to him necessary to play the dandy a little if he were to rouse no suspicions in the lady's breast.

When he arrived at the gate he found it under special police
guard, and as he stepped over the doorway he saw in the distance
a little group of sightseers lingering, despite the frost and an
unfriendly policeman, around the ornate little mansion. It would
have been quicker for him to have gone round to the front of
the flats, but he wanted to find out the communication between
the great house and the small. A few strides took him across
to the back door of the flats, where he almost stumbled over a
woman standing in the doorway chewing sunflower seeds and
spitting out the husks.

"How can I get to flat number 68?" he asked with a well
thought-out blend of courtesy and authority.

Never were nice manners so wasted on a lady. At first he
thought she had not heard him, as she simply went on chewing
and spitting, but just when he contemplated repeating his question, she said without looking at him: "You can't."

"Why not?" he asked with interest.

"You want to go round to the front door in Sand Street."

"But surely it would be quicker for me to go up through the
back stairs, once I'm here," he insisted.

She finished up her fistful of sunflower seeds, freed her hands
of any husks and pieces of grain clinging to them by rubbing
the palms together, spat the last relay of husks over her shoulder
and for the first time looked at her interlocutor.

"You'll have to go right out and along the street and round
the corner," she said with seeming relish at the thought of the
trouble the strange gentleman would be put to. "This is only the
back entrance and there's no numbers on the kitchen doors."

Just then a boy ran down the stairs and through the yard into
the street. The Procurator turned away satisfied. As he had
suspected the back entrance to the flats was used by their inhabitants when their course lay westwards. He strode out of the
yard and into the street with which he was already familiar. A
few steps to the left brought him to a side street which led to
Sand Street, the postal address of the flats he now wished to
enter. The tall building was isolated in the quiet, broad street,
among stuccoed houses of two and three storeys high. Exactly
opposite was a tiny oil shop, at the corner a weeping birch tree.
The picture of provincial peace. The building contained a lift, but
a legend on its door stated that it was not working. As District

Procurator Nikulin mounted the stone staircase he looked about him from left to right for evidence of some way of getting from the main to the back staircase. This was apparently impossible, except through the flats themselves. Number 68 was on the top floor and appeared to harbour five families. A brass plate in the middle of the door advertised a surgeon-dentist by the name of Sokolin. Nikulin rang three times as instructed on the card marked "Burova, Manicurist", and the door was soon opened by a plump little woman holding a wrapper across her bosom. The roaring of a primus stove assaulted his ear. He raised his astrakan cap.

"Would it be convenient for me to have my hands done now?" he asked.

She looked at him helplessly out of a pair of pale blue eyes.

"Oh, yes; quite convenient, if you wouldn't mind waiting five minutes—only five minutes. I've just come in from getting some bread and you know how it is on Sundays, one lies late and there's such a lot to do when you do get up and the girl goes out."

"If it's inconvenient, I'll try and come another time," said the Procurator. "It's too bad to disturb you on a Sunday. But the fact is it's difficult for me to get away during the week."

It was quite obvious the lady wasn't going to let a new client slip through her fingers like that, and she clenched the argument by shutting the door and putting up the chain, disappearing into a room at the end of the passage with a murmured invitation to her visitor to divest himself of his coat. In very little more than five minutes she reappeared, clad in a dress of pale blue silk, and motioning to him coquettishly to follow her. The room into which she led him was small, and stuffed with ornaments, cushions, scent-bottles, statuettes and what-not. A fading hydrangea arose from a fuss of bast bows and frills on a little table, and there were two roses dying in a silver vase. A painted screen ("hand-painted" of course) evidently defended the lady's bed, and seemed to show that her whole life went on in this room, day and night. She made him be seated in a deep armchair, and herself sat on the other side of a little table, covered with the implements of her craft, which she placed between them. She exclaimed with horror when she saw his hands.

"My god, how you have let your nails go!" she cried. "It's

just about time you *did* go to a manicurist! It looks to me as if you'd never been before. But what's the good of cutting them yourself before coming?"

"To tell you the truth, you've guessed right!" he said, with a little laugh, as of shame. "I never *have* been to a manicurist before. But only yesterday a friend of mine told me my nails were a disgrace, and advised me to have them seen to. In fact he gave me your address."

"Really?" He detected the note of interest in her voice. "I wonder who that could have been, now. A lady, I suppose. It isn't often gentlemen come to me."

"But it was a gentleman, just the same," he assured her. "It was my friend Arkady Petrovich Pavlov—"

She interrupted him by a cruel jab in the hand with a sharp instrument, simultaneously emitting a little shriek.

"Arkady Petrovich!" she exclaimed, "do you mean to say you knew him?"

"But of course I know him! I lunched with him only yesterday at the Grand Hotel."

She relinquished his hand, and looked up with frightened blue eyes.

"And you haven't heard?" she gasped.

"Heard what?"

"He's been killed! Murdered in his own room!"

"Why, I saw him only yesterday," said Nikulin, keeping his eyes fixed on her face. "Had dinner with him at the Grand Hotel. You must be mistaken."

"How can I be mistaken, when I saw the police outside the house to-day?" she said. "And the woman who does for me told me all about it herself. He lived just behind here in the yard, you know."

"In this yard?" said Nikulin, in surprised accents. "How can that be? This is Sand Street and he lives—lived—in Little Paul Street—though I've never actually been to his flat."

"But the yard runs between Sand Street and Little Paul Street," she explained. "Oh dear, oh dear, I wish you hadn't mentioned him. I was just beginning to think of something else and now it all comes over me again."

"I'm sincerely sorry," said the Procurator, "I assure you I feel it myself. Dear old Arkady Petrovich! I can't really believe it.

Perhaps you'd rather I left you and came another time about my disgraceful nails."

"Oh, no," she exclaimed, seizing his hands. "Do let me work. It'll help me to forget."

They resumed their former attitudes and she scraped and pushed and filed away in silence, for about two minutes. Then she suddenly began to talk, as the Procurator had hoped she would.

"I'm sure you could have knocked me down with a feather when the girl came in this morning and told me about it," she said. "I happened to be in bed at the time, which was very fortunate for I'm sure I should have fallen down if I had happened to be standing up. I couldn't believe it—why, I saw Arkady Petrovich only the day before yesterday. He was here to have his nails done. Oh dear, such a lovely man! I'm sure a betterhearted man never existed. Everybody loved him, and those poor people downstairs are just in despair, for they'll never get another master like Arkady Petrovich and they know it."

"He was a great-hearted man," said the Procurator solemnly, wishing she wouldn't jab so at the tender skin round the base of his nails.

"That's just what he was," said Miss (or was it Mrs.? he wondered) Burova. "He was an open-handed gentleman. Always a smile for a child and a polite word for a lady. Ah, there's not many left like him in Russia nowadays! But then he lived abroad so long and became a thorough European, so there's no comparison, of course. I shall miss him, I can tell you. I never expect to see another like him."

"Thank you," said the Procurator hastily, "I won't have any of that pink stuff on them."

As he laid a ruble on the table he said carelessly, but watching her face: "By the way, who was it that heard the shot?"

"The shot?" she repeated feebly, with what looked like real bewilderment.

"I mean, who found out about the murder? I suppose somebody heard the shot and gave the alarm."

"Oh, you mean poor Arkady Petrovich," she said, the bewilderment passing like a cloud from her brow. "Oh, didn't I tell you? He wasn't shot at all. Mrs. Stepanovich, that's the night watchman's wife, and she always takes him up his breakfast every morning, you know, so that's how it was she was the first to find it out. Well, she found him stabbed through the heart. And it's thought to be a woman who did it, for some actress was with him last night."

"How do you know it was an actress?" enquired the Procurator.

"Well, if she wasn't an actress, she was no better than she should be," said the manicurist savagely, showing more venom than her mild features had seemed capable of. "Coming home with a man at midnight."

"Why, there's nothing in that nowadays, surely," said the Procurator, surprised at this outburst of puritanism. "I thought it was the usual thing."

"I'm afraid I don't know," was the reply, delivered with distinct acerbity. "*I* always try to remember that I am a lady first and foremost, whatever other people may do."

Feeling distinctly snubbed, the Procurator took his leave with due modesty.

"It wasn't you," he said to himself softly, as he descended the gloomy staircase.

He didn't believe this garrulous, foolish woman knew anything. Those plump hands with glittering nails had thrust no dagger into a man's jugular, of that he felt sure. And if the way she had taken his chance thrust as to the shot was acting, then it was the most marvellous acting he had ever seen.

He returned, full of thought, to his office. That there was a woman in the case he felt pretty sure, but he did not think it was this woman. In the evening he rang up the detective, sent for two men, and sallied forth with them into the snowy street. He hailed a droshky for himself and Yanovitsky, and gave the men instructions to go to the Bolshoï Theatre and wait about as inconspicuously as possible outside the stage-door.

"I've interviewed your soft-hearted lady friend, Yanovitsky," he said to the detective, "and I don't think it was she, somehow, although she admits to having been a friend of Pavlov's, and we may have to call her up to give evidence at the trial. And now we're going to look for quite another lady, as dark as this one is fair."

Yanovitsky grinned his appreciation of his Chief's little joke.

Chapter IV

"...IT WAS YOU..."

IT WAS HALF past eight, and the first interval was just
beginning by the time the two men reached the stage-door of the
Bolshoï Theatre. The Procurator found his way to the office and
inquired for the manager of the ballet department. A heavy,
bearded man moved towards them from the back of the room
and led them into a smaller office opening out of the one they
were at present in.

"District Procurator Nikulin," said the Procurator, introducing
himself.

"Gorbunov—manager of ballet department," murmured the
other.

The Procurator opened his briefcase and took out a dagger and
a tiny screw of paper. Out of the screw of paper he carefully
brought out two tinfoil coins.

"Now, Citizen Gorbunov," he said, "I want to ask you if you
can help us in identifying any of these things. Do you think it's
possible that they come from the wardrobe of the Bolshoï
Theatre?"

Gorbunov leaned forward, adjusting his pince-nez.

"That's more than I can tell you," he said. "Of course, it's
quite possible. But I can take you to someone who will recognise
them if they come from us—identify them at a glance. Or rather
I can of course call her here."

He reached for the telephone standing on the table and gave
an order for Lydia Vassilovna to be sent immediately to the
office.

"Lydia Vassilovna is our Mistress of the Robes," he explained
smiling. "She has been at her post thirty years. She is a most
remarkable lady. I don't suppose there's much that she misses."

While they were waiting for the wardrobe manager to come
the Procurator looked round the tiny office, which was practically
filled by the writing table, a couple of armchairs, and a straight-

backed divan. It seemed to be a room which gave no index to the character of its occupant, excepting that he was probably an untidy man, for the very calendar and the clock were hidden by papers and illustrated magazines, Russian and foreign.

Lydia Vassilovna, when she arrived, looked more like the housekeeper of a country mansion than a stranger would have expected the manageress of a theatrical wardrobe to look. Her hair was smoothed down over her ears and parted in the middle, her plump, white hands folded over her decent black dress. Her calm face expressed surprise at being sent for at such a moment, just when the girls were crowding round her to have a stitch put in here, a piece of torn frilling cut away there, a hook sewn on a bodice—all the minor mishaps that had occurred during the first act. However, she was too dignified to give expression to her surprise and merely stood waiting in the doorway for an order.

Gorbunov showed her the coins and the dagger. She bent forward to examine them. The coins might be from one of her dresses, she said, but the dagger was not theatrical property. It was a real dagger. Asked if she knew which dress she thought the coins came from she said it was likely to be from an eastern costume in "*Prince Igor*".

"Which hasn't been given this week," interpolated Gorbunov.

"No, Alexander Fedorovich, it hasn't," she agreed.

"I should like to put a few questions to Lydia Vassilovna," said the Procurator. "I should like to ask if you ever give costumes out for masquerades or private theatricals."

"That is done sometimes in special circumstances."

"To outsiders? Or to your own actors and actresses only?"

"To both."

Despite her appearance of honesty the Procurator got the impression that this woman was hiding something and purposely keeping her answers as uncommunicative as possible.

"Were any dresses given out in this way during the past week?"

"Yes."

The Procurator refused to show any impatience. If she wasn't in a hurry, he wasn't either.

"Was the dress to which you said these coins might belong thus given out?"

"Yes."

"When?"

"Yesterday."

The atmosphere in the tiny room was tense. All felt that this stout, reserved woman had an important clue in her hands.

"To whom?"

"To one of our young ladies from the ballet."

"Who was it?" rapped out Gorbunov suddenly. "Out with it now, Lydia Vassilovna. It's no use shielding her, it's got to come out."

"To Dolidzey," came the answer, in the same low, toneless voice, but the Procurator, watching closely, thought he saw a look of fear in the steady grey eyes.

Just then an electric bell rang.

"I'm afraid I must ask to see this young lady at once," said the Procurator.

"But they're just preparing to go on," protested Gorbunov. "That bell means the curtain has to go up in three minutes. The next act will be ruined. Dolidzey is one of a group of six to come on immediately."

"I fear the group will have to be of five," said the Procurator inexorably.

"Have you got a warrant for her arrest?" said the other smartly.

"I am furnished with full powers to arrest any person or persons unknown in connection with the murder of Arkady Petrovich Pavlov," said the Procurator quietly, preparing to open his briefcase again.

The wardrobe manageress screamed and caught hold of the back of a chair.

"Tamarachka!" she moaned, pressing a handkerchief to her ashy lips.

Gorbunov hid his face in his hands.

"Murder!" he exclaimed, "Dolidzey? Impossible."

Another bell stabbed the silence.

The Procurator leaned forward and touched Gorbunov sharply on the arm.

"Send for Dolidzey at once," he said, "the third bell will go in a minute, and then it will be too late."

The manager of the ballet department stretched out his hand for the receiver with the strengthless movement of a man who has had a physical shock.

"Send Dolidzey," he said, speaking hoarsely into the receiver. "Gorbunov speaking. Yes, to me. In my office. At once. Never mind. Send her at once, I say. On the stage already? Bring her back. Hold the curtain down for a few minutes and try and send Orlova in her place. If this can't be done, let them go on without her."

He replaced the receiver and the three men and the old woman waited in tense silence, suddenly broken by a violent ring from the telephone, which almost coincided with the third bell for the stage, the bell which sends the audience pouring back from foyer and buffet to crowd into their seats.

"Who?" said Gorbunov wearily. "Vladimir Antonovich? You've sent me Dolidzey? I can't help you, I'm afraid, you must do what you can without her. No, it's no good waiting for her to come back. Get Orlova, or get on without either of them."

He put the receiver back and turned to the Procurator.

"Comrade Procurator," he said. "Who has been murdered? Who is Pavlov? And why is Dolidzey, a young girl in her teens, suspected?"

Before the Procurator could answer, the door suddenly opened, and a young girl, in the traditional ballet-dress, short, gauzy skirt and long pink legs, came in. The Procurator covered the dagger with a newspaper with a swift movement. All faces were involuntarily turned towards the young girl, but before they had time to take in her appearance a young man with pale face and disordered hair came headlong into the room, and taking not the slightest notice of any of the strangers rushed up to the manager of the ballet department and began to hammer on the desk with his fists.

"Alexander Fedorovich!" he exclaimed. "This is impossible! They're calling out in the theatre for the curtain to go up and you keep back Dolidzey at the last moment. I can't keep the curtain down another second. It's impossible."

"I told you to get Orlova if you could," said Gorbunov.

The young man seemed to go almost mad with impatience.

"Alexander Fedorovich," he said reproachfully, "you know Orlova can't be dressed and made up in five minutes, especially when you keep Lydia Vassilovna. Besides, she's in the club. It would take ten minutes to find her."

Gorbunov raised his hand and the Procurator observed that it was freshly manicured, like his own, but with a fine pink gloss on each polished nail. "That's what mine would have been like if I'd let that woman mess them up with her pink stuff," he thought involuntarily, but immediately focused his attention again on the duel going on between the two men.

"Go and get your curtain up," Gorbunov was saying calmly. "Dolidzey must stay here. She cannot go back."

With a wild look from the manager to the motionless girl, and a stare of curiosity at the strangers, the young man turned on his heel and disappeared from the room.

"Come here, Tamara Geyorgyevna," said Gorbunov, pulling forward a chair almost opposite to the Procurator. "Comrade Nikulin wishes to ask you a few questions."

The girl looked from one to another from heavy black eyes. She was made up for the stage, with spots of garish red in the corners of her blue-ringed eyes, and in her nostrils. Under the paint her young face looked drawn.

"Did you take a dress from the wardrobe yesterday?"

"Yes," came the low reply.

"Do these two coins belong to it?"

"I don't know."

"Might they have?"

"Yes."

"Did you return the dress to the theatre?"

"Not yet. I haven't had time."

"Did you wear a dagger with this dress?"

"Yes."

"Where is it?"

An almost imperceptible pause.

"At home."

"Are you sure?"

"Of course."

"Thank you. Then you will perhaps be so good as to go home and fetch it. By the way, you're sure this isn't it?"

With a sudden movement the Procurator removed the newspaper with which he had hidden the dagger when the girl entered the room. She stared at it with dilated eyes and seemed to shrink back into herself.

"Blood!" she exclaimed. "Oh, no, no, it's not my dagger! It can't be mine!"

"Well, perhaps you'll go and fetch us yours, and then we shall be quite sure," said the Procurator. "Inspector Yanovitsky here will accompany you and help you to find it."

The girl looked helplessly at Gorbunov.

"Can't I change my clothes and wipe off the grease-paint?" she faltered.

The old woman in the chair made a movement as if to help her that seemed almost as instinctive as the hen's spreading of her wings over her chicks.

But the Procurator held up an inhibitory hand.

"I'm afraid I can't allow you to leave the room without Inspector Yanovitsky," he said. "But Lydia Vassilovna can go and fetch your own clothes, and a cloth or something to wipe your face."

The old woman rose with a long, quivering sigh, and left the room. She was back again in about five minutes, during which nobody spoke, and the girl sat gazing before her with her tragic eyes in their lurid rings of blue grease-paint. When Lydia Vassilovna returned, her arms heaped with clothes, Nikulin rose.

"I am going back to my office," he said. "Yanovitsky, you will accompany Tamara Geyorgyevna to her house and bring her to me with whatever you may find, later. Lydia Vassilovna, perhaps you will find time to come and see me to-morrow morning before going to the theatre. There are still one or two questions I should like to put to you."

"If I can be of any use, Comrade Procurator," said Gorbunov, rising and extending his plump hand.

"Thank you, I shall probably have to ask you to come and see me later," said Nikulin. "Now, perhaps we had all better go into the next room, to allow Tamara Geyorgyevna to change her clothes. I'm afraid Inspector Yanovitsky will have to remain here."

"I won't look," said that gentleman good-humouredly.

Nikulin then took his leave, ascertaining on his way out that the sledge still stood at the door and that his escort was in sight. He asked them to try not to look quite so obvious, a request that the honest lads ill understood, to get another sledge and follow Inspector Yanovitsky and the girl. He himself took a tram and returned to a well-earned supper, not displeased with his success, but not without pity for the young thing he had so unexpectedly found in his trap.

About ten minutes later Yanovitsky came out of the stage door, followed by the girl Dolidzey in an almost fainting condition.

Alone with a young girl Inspector Yanovitsky became something more than the respectful automaton with a villainous glance. His bright, hard eye softened perceptibly, he twirled his fierce moustache unconsciously, and his hand seemed to hover about the girl's elbow, as if it would gladly support it, but wished not to be forward. When, however, they came to the sledge at the kerb he gave expression to his feeling of goodwill to all women by a hearty heaving of the young girl on to the seat.

"Now you make yourself comfortable, my dear," he said, "and don't worry, that's the main thing."

"Come on, you fellows," he cried to the men climbing into the other sledge, "now don't you lose sight of us, you're here to take care of us, you know. And now we're off."

Not all his good humour could get a word out of the girl who sat bundled up in her corner with averted head. She had told him her address when he asked for it and she seemed not to have another word in her. The sledges crossed the great square in front of the theatre and entered the Red Square through the sacred Ivor Gate, the holiest shrine in Moscow, the driver of the front sledge pulling off his shaggy cap and crossing himself; he in the one which followed with the escort paying no heed whatsoever to the shrine, but never ceasing to cluck to his horses and exchange pleasantries with the two young men in the narrow sledge. They passed the Church of St. Basil the Blessed, slid down the steep slope to the river and walked at a foot pace across the bridge. This soon brought them to the poorer quarter of the town, and here, after a few minutes sliding over the smooth, hardened snow, the front driver drew up at a corner house, grim, tall and narrow. Yanovitsky got out, helped the girl out, and instructed the escort to remain at the door. At a word from the detective the girl produced a key from her pocket and silently admitted him. She led him up a dark stairway to a door on the fourth landing, which she opened with another key from her pocket. The room was desolate and comfortless. A naked electric bulb, much in need of substitution by a new one, shed a sickly glare over the poor appointments. A high narrow bed supported the bodies of two persons, one of whom turned an old lean face, sticking out of a wadded crimson quilt like the head of a giant tortoise from its shell, when the door opened. The other showed nothing but tufts of lamp-black hair. For the rest the chamber was coldly furnished with rolls and cylinders of leather, black and brown, filling the air with its strong, slightly sickening smell, a cobbler's bench, rough, dark tools against the wall, three wooden chairs, a deal table holding a tin basin and the ubiquitous primus stove, and practically nothing else. One corner was curtained off by a rich, dark red carpet depending from a sagging rod about five foot from the floor. Yanovitsky was incapable of appreciating the beauty of this noble rug, but he was not slow to estimate its probable value, for even he could see that those birds and trees and butterflies, those buff and blue and purple snakes, could only have taken life on the looms of Persia.

Leaving the detective at the door Tamara stepped swiftly up to the bed and began to speak to the old female tortoise in a rapid guttural torrent of words of which Yanovitsky could understand nothing at all. Whatever she told her it distressed the old lady, who began to lift up her voice and shake her sleeping partner by the shoulder. The black head stirred on the pillow and up hove a pair of mighty shoulders in a striped shirt. Next a red face with an immense curved nose, beetling brows and eaves-like moustache came into view. When he saw that mighty torso, Yanovitsky, who was no coward, could not help thinking involuntarily of his escort at the door. But the man seemed to have no intention of leaving his bed, and when the detective after searching the bare room minutely, asked him to get up and allow him to search the bed, he got out quietly and shambled on to the floor without a word. His search of the chamber, which was rendered easier by the scrupulous neatness with which everything in the poor room was kept, yielded little that was to his purpose, but that little was very much to his purpose—to wit, the empty scabbard of a Caucasian dagger. For the rest he took a shabby gipsy costume over his arm and was instructing the girl to accompany him out of the room when with a quick spring she dashed over to the curtained off corner before he could stop her and was back again at his side like lightning with a small wad of notes in her hand. The astonished detective thought at first that she was going to try and bribe him, but as she merely stuffed them into her pocket he refrained from questioning her. That would be the business of his chief. But when he would have left the room with Tamara the old crone set up such a deafening lamentation and recrimination in scarcely intelligible Russian that Yanovitsky's gentleness suddenly broke down and he burst out into the coarse and brutal reviling that was his only method of dealing with opposition. The old man, beyond a few sorrowful words in the Georgian language to Tamara, said nothing, and this alone prevented the detective from resorting to actual force to get the girl away. As it was, there was a painful scene at the last moment in which Yanovitsky tore the skinny, claw-like hands of the old woman from the girl's arms and pushed Tamara before him through the door. The old woman's wailing and recriminations accompanied them down the stairs until they emerged into the quiet night. The whole way to the police station Tamara, who had shrunk from the detective's touch when the latter tried, with a resumption of his former gallantry, to help her into the sledge, relapsed into profound silence, almost seeming to hold her breath.

The sledges slid silently over the snow, and in about fifteen minutes they arrived outside the district police station. The girl allowed herself to be shepherded in with no more protest than an agonised backward look at the street, rather as if she thought she would never see the light of day again. Yanovitsky paid and dismissed both drivers and, leaving his escort in the outer office, ushered his trembling prey into the office of the District Procurator.

After hearing the detective's report, the Procurator dismissed his subordinate, and hunter and victim were left face to face and alone. But seldom did hunter feel less triumph or more distress, and gladly would the Procurator have postponed the ordeal through which he was bound to pass the trembling young creature before him. There was, however, nothing for it and he coughed, lit a cigarette, arranged and rearranged his papers on the desk in front of him, before making up his mind to raise his eyes to the girl on the other side of the desk.

Perhaps he would not have recognised in the ill-dressed, dusky-skinned girl before him the painted ballet girl of a few hours back, if he did not still remember so poignantly the great, heavy black eyes in the blue-white shining whites. She now wore a creased blouse of black sateen, grey with constant, but not apparently very recent laundering, over a short skirt of rubbed brown serge. The Procurator's trained eye noted a missing button at the neck and the belt was tied in a clumsy knot instead of being buckled. Her short thick hair lacked gloss, and her heavy boots were patched. A poor girl, evidently a very poor girl.

The Procurator already had before him the fruits of Yanovitsky's search: the fancy dress (which Lydia Vassilovna had reluctantly testified to lack four coins, one of which had already been missing, so that, with the two found in the dead man's room, only one was unaccounted for); the scabbard of a dagger, into which that drawn from the dead man's jugular fitted exactly, one hundred rubles in ten-ruble notes. All these trophies lay before the Procurator on his desk, with the exception of the costume, a poor flimsy affair in gaudy colours, which hung over the back of a chair beside him.

"Now, Tamara," said Nikulin familiarly, lighting a cigarette, "you just keep perfectly calm, and tell me all you know about these things found in your room. First of all, this dress: when did you wear it?"

"Last night."

"Where?"

"At Pavlov's house."

"What were you doing there?"

"He asked me to come and dance for his guests."

"How many guests were there?"

"I don't know."

"At a rough guess?"

"About fifteen or twenty, I suppose."

"Who played accompaniments?"

"I don't know."

"Now, my good girl, what's the use of saying things like that?" said the Procurator in accents of paternal reproach. "If somebody played your accompaniments, you must have seen him, you know, and you must even have spoken to him."

"I mean I don't know who he was. I never saw him before."

"Well, all right. Now what instrument did he play? Fiddle? Piano?"

"Piano."

"So. Piano. Well now, about this dagger? Will you admit now that it's yours? We've found the scabbard, you know, and it fits perfectly."

The girl started.

"It has blood on it!" she cried. "I never killed anybody. I never touched him with the dagger!"

"But if there were no blood on it, would you then admit that it was yours?"

"It's like mine."

"You didn't find yours at home?"

"No, I couldn't."

"Tamara, this is your dagger."

"Well, all right, it is," came the sulky answer. "But I never touched anyone with it all the same."

"Now, that's better. If you only tell the truth we shall get along ever so much better. Now just tell me how your dagger came to be in Pavlov's room."

"I might have dropped it."

"Did you?"

"I might have."

"All right, then, you might have dropped it. Now what about this hundred rubles you have brought with you?"

In his report Yanovitsky had described the girl's last action before leaving the room.

"He gave it to me for dancing. I said it was too much, but he made me take it."

"You didn't take any more?"

"No. I didn't want to take that. I said it was too much, but he made me."

"All right. Now then, what time did you leave Pavlov's rooms? Or rather, first of all tell me when you got there."

"About twelve."

"How do you know what the time was?"

"Because he came round for me after the theatre and by the time I had my make-up washed off and the other costume on, it must have been nearly twelve."

"And when did you leave Pavlov's room?"

"I don't know, but when I passed the clock in the Kremlin it was striking the quarter."

"The quarter—?"

"I mean a quarter past one."

"How long did it take you to walk to the Red Square? You walked there?"

"Yes."

"Where do you live?"

"On the Balchug."

"That would take you about twenty minutes from Little Paul Street?"

"Fifteen. I walk fast."

"You walk fast. All right. But you must have left Pavlov's rooms a little before one, for you had to get to the gate first, and the distance must be at least fifteen minutes from door to door, even for a quick walker. But you say you heard the clock strike the quarter when you were in the Red Square. So you may of course have left the room precisely at one or a few minutes after. That means your dancing must have been over at least by twenty to one, allowing for you to change and put on your goloshes, and so on, even if Pavlov didn't give you a sandwich and a drink, which he must surely have done."

"He wanted to, but I wouldn't."

"Why not?"

"I wanted to get home. I didn't like being there."

"And that is all you have to say to me?"

"Yes."

"Well, now, Tamara, I have something to say to you. This morning Pavlov was found dead with this dagger—your dagger, Tamara—in his neck. Nobody is known to have come to him but yourself *and nobody was there but yourself, Tamara.* Nobody played your accompaniments on a piano because there was no piano in the room. There were no other guests. You were alone with Pavlov between twelve and one, and between twelve and three Pavlov was killed—with your dagger, Tamara."

The girl listened to him with distended eyes and rapidly paling cheeks. She became so ashen white that the Procurator looked around for a glass of water, but suddenly the colour came back into her cheeks in hot waves.

"Pavlov killed!" she exclaimed. "But he can't be! I—he—I was talking to him last night, he was alive, he was well, eating, drinking, I never—"

She clutched at the neck of her dress as if she had difficulty in breathing.

"Have you anything more to tell me?" asked the Procurator inexorably.

"I didn't kill him, I didn't. I didn't touch him! He was alive when I left! He was pouring himself out a glass of vodka."

"But this is your dagger."

"Yes, yes, it is! It's my dagger! But I never touched him! I dropped it, I couldn't find it! I didn't touch him!"

Interested in her remark that she had dropped the dagger and been unable to find it, the Procurator tried cross-examination, but she fell suddenly silent, her hand on her head, only emitting a low moan every now and then, and the Procurator judged it would be useless to persist in the cross-examination just then.

CHAPTER V

THEATRICAL

NEXT MORNING THE Procurator sent for the wardrobe mistress. The old lady was as severe-looking and composed as ever, and answered all his questions with dignity and precision.

"Did you know yesterday that this dagger belonged to Dolidzey?"

"How could I know? All daggers are alike. I didn't think about it?"

"It will be hard for you to convince me that you did not think about it. Why did you not tell me that you had reason to believe that it belonged to Dolidzey?"

"You didn't ask me," was the calm reply.

"That is not why. You wished to shield Dolidzey. Why?"

"I—we are all—very fond of Dolidzey," answered the old woman with the first emotion she had shown. "She is the best girl I ever had in the school. I didn't like her going to Pavlov's last night. I felt no good would come of it."

"Oh, so you knew she was going?"

"Yes, she told me herself. She said: 'Auntie Lidochka, a rich old speculator has asked me to go and dance for his guests. Should I go, do you think?'"

"Did you try to discourage her?"

"Yes, I did, sir! I know what a lighthearted little thing she is, and I don't think she knows how wicked life is. I didn't trust this Pavlov. I never did."

"Did you know him?"

"No, but I heard the girls talking about him. He was always hanging about the stage door and trying to get Tamara— Dolidzey—to go with him."

"And what can you tell me about the dagger?"

"It's hers, Tamara's. I knew that from the beginning and now it's well known, there's no use concealing it. She was all ready dressed to go and one of the other young ladies said: 'You need a dagger, Tamara. Lydia Vassilovna will give you one if you ask her.' And she answered up: 'I don't need your wretched cardboard daggers. I've got a proper Caucasian kinjal.' "

"Were there others present when she said this?"

"Yes. Several of the girls were standing round, and I think one of the boys, but I'm not sure."

"Can you name me any of these?"

The old woman hesitated, then seemed to make up her mind that the information might as well come from her as another.

"There was Matveyeva and Goldstein, and, I think, Kuznetzova—all young ones."

The Procurator made a note of the names.

"What else can you remember of the conversation?"

"Oh, I had my work to do," said the old woman, her voice suddenly cold. "I didn't take that much notice of their idle chatter."

Nikulin felt that she had heard more that she did not care to repeat, but he was not inclined to press her. He would get his information more easily out of the young ones. He sent for them without, however, releasing Lydia Vassilovna, half afraid that she might see fit to give them some warning. The old woman sighed deeply once, but made no other sign of life during the whole of the three quarters of an hour which she had to wait.

Liza Matveyeva turned out to be much more the traditional ballerina than Tamara. She was slight and blonde, with legs already beginning to become set and muscular, as they always do with tip-toe dancers. She was elegant in a rather cheap sort of way, and carried a handbag with the fashionable zip fastener that was something of a wonder in Moscow, at that time.

"Tamara was all ready dressed to go and one of the other young ladies said: 'You need a dagger, Tamara,' " read the Procurator from the notes he had made of his conversation with Lydia Vassilovna. "Who said it? Was it you?"

The girl cocked her pretty head on one side, pouting and frowning reflectively. At last she wasn't sure. She might have and again she might not have. Somebody said it, but she couldn't swear if it had been she or another.

"What did Dolidzey say to this?"

"I can't remember her exact words, but I know she said she didn't need one because she had a real one of her own."

"Did she say: 'I don't need your wretched cardboard daggers. I've got a proper Caucasian kinjal'?"

"Yes," said the girl eagerly, and she said: 'And I know how to use it, too.' I remember, because we all laughed."

The Procurator turned to the wardrobe mistress.

"You remember that, Lydia Vassilovna?"

"I couldn't say, I'm sure," answered the old woman with compressed lips. "I've got more to do than listen to young people's chatter, let alone treasure it up."

But she shot a glance full of venom at Matveyeva, which inclined the Procurator to think that she recognised the remark.

"Can you tell me anything more that was said?" he went on, to the obliging Matveyeva.

"I think one of the girls said—asked her—if she could kill anyone by sticking the dagger through their heart, and then Dubinski said: 'Stick it through my heart, Tamara, to show them. You've slain me long ago, anyhow, so you might as well.' And Tamara laughed and said that's not the way to do it."

The other girls when questioned corroborated practically all Matveyeva's statements. Only Dubinsky, the young man reported to have made burlesque love to Tamara, professed entire ignorance of the whole incident. When asked how it was that his memory appeared to be so much weaker than that of the girls, he replied with a sneer that perhaps it was not his memory, but merely his imagination that was weaker. The Procurator felt pretty sure, however, that this was a mere vain attempt at chivalry.

The next caller—by self-invitation—was the manager of the ballet school, Gorbunov. His report on Dolidzey was practically confirmation of everybody else's. Singular unanimity seemed to prevail about this girl who, in the five years in which she had been at the school, had become a general favourite.

"It distresses me, Comrade Procurator," said Gorbunov, mopping at his brow. The Procurator had already noticed the man's tendency to ooze at the pores. He noted that the man was a typical apoplectic—stout, soft-bodied and short in the neck. It was clear that his distress was quite genuine.

"It distresses me more than I can say," repeated Gorbunov. "Of course that's natural. It's distressing in itself that any of our charges should be involved in such a terrible affair, but it's particularly distressing that it should be Dolidzey. Such a good girl, Procurator, and such a talent! Ah! What a talent! A budding Pavlova, I assure you, but with a fiery eastern temperament that Pavlova lacks."

"You consider her temperament fiery?" said the Procurator.

"Fiery!" said Gorbunov emphatically. "Fiery, Comrade Procurator. Why, the girl's a volcano of potential passions. I shouldn't care to be in the shoes of any man who roused the anger of that young woman!"

"Interesting to hear you say so," said the Procurator, carelessly, "for other witnesses testify to perpetual good humour and turning aside all unpleasantnesses with laughter."

"Superficial judgment, Comrade Nikulin! Superficial! Superficial! I keep my eyes open as I go about the school, and I have had this girl under special observation for five years, ever since she came to the school at the age of twelve—a grotesque little imp with a cropped head and raw elbows. I've kept her under observation because of her exceptional talent, which I was the first to discover. I've seen many a young fellow wilt under the blaze of those black eyes, I have indeed, Procurator. A volcano, I assure you! A volcano."

"Did you know of her acquaintance with Pavlov?" inquired the Procurator.

Gorbunov pursed up his lips and shook his head.

"I did not," he said. "Had I known of it, this deplorable incident would not have occurred, for I should have done my best to discourage it."

"Why? Did you know the man?"

"I knew *of* him, of course, as an amateur of the ballet. My profession brings me in touch with strange people, Comrade Procurator, very strange people, I assure you."

"But were you acquainted with him personally?" pursued the Procurator.

"I may have exchanged a few words with him at one time or another. He came to the theatre so frequently, and of course got an introduction to me. In fact once or twice I remember obtaining for him a couple of stalls for the ballet, though he generally got them in the usual way through the box office, I believe, paying for them, of course. Yes, Comrade Procurator, my profession brings me in contact with strange people. Beggars can't be choosers, you know. Of course we ourselves might prefer to have dealings with none but workers and peasants, but beggars can't be choosers, you know."

The Procurator shot an amused glance at the man's white, well cared for hands, and thought he knew how Gorbunov would deal with the workers and peasants if beggars *could* be choosers. He was half-amused, half-disgusted at the man's disclaimer of acquaintance with the murdered Pavlov, but it was no more than he had expected. He had known there would be few to claim the friendship of the convivial Pavlov, once dead, more especially since he had been murdered. And yet he felt pretty sure there had been more than a nodding acquaintance between the two men, for he had seen in Gorbunov's office quite a recent copy of the same Parisian journal that he had noticed on the dead man's writing table, and it seemed to him that only men who were fairly intimate, or at least had a good mutual understanding, would borrow such journals from each other. That they might independently have been subscribers he dismissed as far-fetched, for such literature is not received through the open post in Moscow. No, Pavlov must have had access to some privileged means of communication—perhaps a friend attached to some embassy—for getting the literature in which his soul delighted, and it was at least highly likely to have been he who lent it to Gorbunov.

Not wishing, however, to embarrass the ballet manager with his inconvenient suspicions, for he wanted him to answer a few more questions freely and openly, the Procurator kept his speculations to himself.

"In your opinion then," he continued, "Dolidzey is a girl capable of sticking a knife into a man if he annoyed her."

"Not if he annoyed her, Comrade Procurator! Not annoyed. That is not enough. But let a man attack her honour, and I wouldn't give much for his chances! Like many truly passionate natures, fiercely virginal, Comrade Procurator, fiercely virginal."

"Then your theory is that he tried to take her by force, and she struggled and took out her dagger in self-defence."

"I'm sure of it, convinced of it, Comrade Procurator!" said the other importantly. "That must have been how the whole distressing incident occurred."

"And the empty pocket-book on the writing table? How about that?"

Gorbunov shook his head ruefully.

"Ah, I hadn't heard about that. I didn't know there was any question of money involved. That looks bad. Very bad. And not like Dolidzey as we knew her. Comrade Procurator, I would have answered for that girl's honesty with my life. I would indeed."

"All right," said the Procurator, with the first impatience he had yet shown during the interview, though by no means with the first he had felt, for the ballet manager seemed to him an exasperating canting sort of fellow, and his constantly reiterated "Comrade Procurator" was beginning to get on that gentleman's nerves. "But you see yourself that in view of the empty pocket-book and the hundred rubles to which Dolidzey herself owns, the defence of honour story hardly holds good. It doesn't seem likely that a man would present a girl with a hundred rubles *before* proceeding to ravish her."

"Wait a bit, Comrade Procurator," interrupted Gorbunov, an admonitory finger raised. "Wait a bit. It holds, it holds. Let us say the girl struggles in the villain's arms. She gives a quick involuntary thrust at him, the jugular is pierced, the man falls at her feet a corpse. Horrified, she looks round for flight. Her eyes fall on the open pocket-book on the table. Money! The means for flight, the only means! Half instinctively, she sweeps up the notes and flies."

"And yet you would answer for her honesty with your life!" said the Procurator drily.

"In normal moments, Comrade Procurator, in normal moments. In moments of crisis it is impossible to answer for anyone, for we cannot answer for ourselves. Besides, having committed a murder, however involuntarily, it doesn't seem so very serious to take a few notes. Mark my words, you'll find it has been as I say: she loses her head, she gathers up the money, she flies."

"Very good," said the Procurator. "But if she stabbed him while struggling in his arms, why was she not covered with blood from the jugular?"

Gorbunov was silent.

"Moreover there was no struggle," continued the Procurator steadily. "Pavlov was killed in cold blood, while he was changing a gramophone record. That doesn't sound much like a struggle for honour, does it?"

Beads of sweat broke out on the ballet manager's temples. He produced an ample handkerchief and mopped his brow again and again. This information had obviously been a horrid shock to his sensibilities.

"You don't say so!" he exclaimed. "Why that's terrible, Comrade Nikulin. Terrible! Changing a gramophone record, you say?"

"He had just put the needle in position to begin a new record. It was wound up, and even went on revolving when the weight of the body—the head, was removed from it."

"Ghastly! Ghastly!" muttered Gorbunov, with another dab at his forehead. "I was visualising all the time a struggle in self-defence, but you have made me see it as a cold-blooded murder for theft. Ghastly, ghastly! And the record went on revolving after—Ugh!"

"Queasy fellow!" thought the Procurator, watching him closely. "Can't stand hearing about horrors. He might find workers and peasants a bit strong for his nerves. Or did he really know Pavlov intimately, and do the details affect him because of that?"

"But I understood you to say there was a struggle," continued Gorbunov, breaking in upon the Procurator's reflections. "You said so, I'm sure you did."

"I said nothing of the sort," said Nikulin.

"Why, you brought along two sequins which you said were torn off in a struggle."

"*Might* have been torn off in a struggle," corrected the Procurator. "There may have been a struggle, but if so it was over, and the strugglers had kissed and made friends. For Pavlov was playing the gramophone for his own, or somebody else's entertainment."

Gorbunov's "ghastly, ghastly", again reiterated had already become a little automatic, and it was obvious he was pursuing some other line of thought.

"But still I don't quite give my theory up," he suddenly said in quite a different voice. "After all, there may have been a struggle. Let us say that he tried to embrace her forcibly. She repulses him. He pretends to give in—out of strategy, mind you, mere strategy. He gets out the gramophone to throw dust in her eyes by making her think he is going to offer her innocent entertainment, but says something so cynical while placing the record on, that the blood rushes to her head and she lunges at him before she knows what she is doing."

"Hum," said the Procurator, not much impressed.

"I wish I could see her," said the other suddenly, as if struck by a new idea. "I feel sure I could get her to confess exactly what happened."

"What makes you think so?"

"She has confidence in me. She knows I wish her well. She might tell me what she wouldn't tell you—a stranger and an official."

"Sorry, impossible."

The Procurator rose to signify that the interview was over.

CHAPTER VI

THE LATE MR. PAVLOV

INQUIRIES ABOUT PAVLOV were not particularly illuminating. Very little more was learned than his papers had revealed. He was the manager of the Moscow branch of Obless timber concession in Siberia. He had a sister in New York, who had cabled that she was sending attested material by post, and the friend inquiring about a Russian *visa* had given a satisfactory account of himself from Paris. In Pavlov's office he had found no private papers of any sort, and his banking account showed that he had drawn no great sum of money lately, not more than could have been accounted for by daily expenses, and perhaps three hundred rubles in hand. Of these, one hundred had been found in the possession of Dolidzey, and there remained a hypothetical two hundred which might, of course, never have existed, although it scarcely seemed likely that a man would give away all his ready cash to the last kopek—especially on a Saturday night! If he had intended to give the girl a hundred rubles, surely he would have set it aside from another sum! Besides there was the evidence of the empty note-case on the writing table. True, if Dolidzey were a thief, she had shown extreme cunning in reserving (and accounting for) a hundred rubles, and getting rid of the rest. Indeed the latter feat practically argued the presence of an accomplice.

As far as the Procurator could make out from the usual chorus of praise that is sung over the dead, Pavlov had been one of those typical Russians in whom charity covers a multitude of sins. He pictured him as an easy, sensual man, living only for himself but gifted with that good humour and urbanity which is so often preferred by society to the sterner virtues. Apparently the man had divided his time between his office, the theatres and few hotels of Moscow and—his one great passion—the ballet. But conviviality is uneasy in modern Russia, and if he had had boon companions they were slow to come forward, afraid, evidently, to expose themselves to the glare of publicity. If there were maîtres d'hôtels and head waiters who had seen him often with the same companions they managed to forget.

As to his presence in Moscow, that was easily accounted for. The timber concession was in the hands of an American firm, for which Pavlov's father had formerly worked. Pavlov had been in America, on business for the firm when the March revolution broke out, and he had stayed there. When, however, the concession was again put into the hands of its old owners, Pavlov had been sent out as manager of the Moscow branch, and no objection had been made on the part of Moscow. The family was from Siberia and appeared to have few connections in Moscow or Leningrad.

The small staff at the dead man's office appeared to be plunged in deepest gloom by the sudden and shocking end of their chief. The Procurator attributed this partly to the loss of a chief of real good nature and pleasant ways—no stickler for undue discipline and not a petty-souled man to stipulate for rigid punctuality, or look too closely into a ruble here and a ruble there from the petty cash for a droshky to catch the post, or make a fuss about his employees being called frequently to the office telephone; partly also he could not help putting it down to natural fears of losing a very comfortable job, for as every office employee knows, changes at the top are only too likely to bring with them changes at the bottom, and new brooms are apt to sweep out ruthlessly many a comfortable soul that had deemed itself safe for life.

All agog as he was to find the possible woman in the case, the Procurator had to admit that there did not seem to be any in Pavlov's office. Whatever may have been his weaknesses with regard to women, Pavlov evidently belonged to the ranks of those gentlemen who allow caution to override feeling in business, and believe a plain stenographer likely to be more efficient than a pretty one. Perhaps stern experience had taught him this, or perhaps he had been unable to find a female secretary who should combine all the virtues with a few at least of the graces. Be that as it may, Miss Gregoriev was uncompromisingly plain, and at least forty. The Procurator could only hope that she was efficient in inverse ratio to her charms. She had little to tell him beyond the fact that she had been working as the dead man's secretary and stenographer for two years—ever since the Moscow office of the Obless had been opened, in fact—that she knew nothing of his personal life, had never seen him out of the office, and had certainly never been to his room. All of which the Procurator had no difficulty in believing. Other members of the office staff were an elderly book-keeper and an office boy, neither of whom seemed to have anything particularly illuminating to tell the Procurator, and both of whom struck him as eminently respectable and unsuspicious persons. The boy testified to having been sent out pretty frequently to secure theatre tickets and on the day of the murder itself he had been dispatched to buy flowers, fruit and a box of chocolates, all of which the Procurator felt certain had been destined to grace the supper table on the fateful night.

Among the dead man's papers three half sheets were found with the beginnings of evidently discarded letters upon them. One began: "My dear Miss Dolidzey", crossed out, another: "Dear little dancing girl", and the third: "Dear Tamara Geyorgyevna". Evidently neither form of address had satisfied the writer, for in each case they had been crossed out and the letters not continued. They all bore the same date—three days before the day of the murder. This was the only evidence of real importance that Pavlov's office yielded, although of course he was able to establish a great many facts about the dead man's life and connections. Another photographic group on the wall, of men in overalls and blouses, posed about a great load of timber on a truck, proved to have been taken at the same time as the companion picture that the Procurator had noted in the dead man's own room and bore the same date and inscription, but nothing else in the austere office reminded the Procurator of the far from austere rooms he had just visited, until he found, in the only locked drawer in the whole desk, a packet of picture post-cards—also of Parisian origin. This was valuable in contributing with strong logic towards the general portrait of the murdered man that was gradually forming itself in the Procurator's mind, but it did little to furnish any real clues. The unwritten letters to the girl Dolidzey did but confirm information the Procurator already had as to their relations—at least on the man's side— just as the postcards, in their puerile crudity, confirmed the opinion he had formed of Pavlov as a banal *bon vivant*, a survival of the class that has gone under in Russia. But nothing more definite was forthcoming, after the most painstaking search had been undertaken, and investigations positively artistic in their thoroughness had been carried through.

None of the staff made the slightest objection to their finger-prints being taken and none of the finger-prints proved to be of the slightest use to the Procurator who emerged, weary and unsatisfied, after hours of practically fruitless work.

By the time he found himself once again out in the snowy street it seemed to the Procurator more certain than ever that the ballet girl Dolidzey had been guilty of the murder of the business man Pavlov, whether from mctives of revenge, for theft, or both, he was not as yet satisfied. And being human he could not help feeling a little sorry. It seemed to him a pity that a fresh young life should have come to grief over anything so flat, stale and unprofitable as the late Mr. Pavlov.

CHAPTER VII

ENTER THE PRESS

ON LEAVING HIS room the next day the Procurator almost stumbled over a small man with a large head, whom he recognised somewhat ruefully as a correspondent of the *Moskovskaya Zvezda* (*The Moscow Star*), an evening paper that was making valiant efforts to distribute the benefits of culture as understood by western European journalism.

"Ah, Julius Cæsarovich!" exclaimed Nikulin, making a virtue of necessity by greeting the little man with some show of a cordiality he was far from feeling at the moment. Not that he or anybody else had anything but liking for Mr. Itkin, Julius the son of Cæsar, but like all officials he hated his cases to get into the press before he was through with them, and regarded journalists as a whole as a pestilent race.

"What wind blows you in?" he cried, with a somewhat false gaiety. "Or, rather, perhaps I should say what makes you gentlemen of the press get wind of just what you're not meant to?"

"Citizen District Procurator!" said the little man, with a bow of mock gravity. "Comrade Nikulin! Respected Andrei Mihailovich! A very good morning to you! I only ask for five minutes about the Pavlov case."

"I have nothing for you to put in that rag of yours, if that's what you're after," said the Procurator drily.

"Ah, but supposing I'm after helping *you*," said the little man, with the imperturbable good humour that made him the most successful stunt journalist in the U.S.S.R. "Suppose Julius Cæsarovich can get hold of the street boys who were seen to enter the yard, but were not seen to leave it? Aha, Mr. Procurator! What then! Is it worth a ten minutes' chat for the *Moskovskaya Zvezda*?"

The Procurator hesitated.

"Do you really know anything, Itkin?" he asked.

"Not just now, but I will soon," returned Itkin placidly. "Or if I don't, then you know no one else will, as far as street boys are concerned."

The Procurator was silent. He knew that it was no idle boast, for Julius Cæsarovich had the run and the confidence of the Moscow underworld. He began to think over for the hundredth time the two boys seen by the night watchman to enter the yard. The man had said he saw them most nights, and never saw them return, but an examination of the yard showed that it would have been a comparatively easy matter (for a boy) to leave it by scrambling on to the top of a wood shed against the wall, while to get *into* the yard in the same way would have presented serious difficulties, it being a great deal easier to drop from a sheer wall than to scale it. The boys had not been traced, and the Procurator felt pretty sure that it would be impossible to trace them, at any rate for the police.

"Come on in," he said wearily, turning slowly back towards his office. "I might be inclined for once to break my rule and answer a few questions, on condition that you don't come back here without some information about those boys."

"I may not as yet know anything—I say I *may* not—I am certainly not as yet in a position to give you any definite information. But if I don't find out something to-day about those boys I shall to-morrow, and that's more than you can confidently assert yourself, isn't it, Mr Procurator?"

"It certainly is," admitted Nikulin ruefully.

"You have, I presume, made certain efforts to have these unknown, but well-attested boys followed up," continued the journalist, his voice heavy with sarcasm.

The Procurator made a gesture of despair.

"Follow up street boys!" he said. "You know yourself the thing's impossible! But Yanovitsky is satisfied that none of the windows has been entered—and you would hardly expect street boys to go in by the front door, would you?"

"Yanovitsky is a—well, never mind! Those boys have forgotten more than Yanovitsky ever knew. But trust Julius Cæsarovich, Procurator! You know there's hardly a street urchin in Moscow that I haven't played pitch and toss with, not a prison which does not shelter one or other of my very good friends. In fact, you know Julius Cæsarovich Itkin, you know his tastes; in a word you know your case could not be in better hands."

The Procurator smiled at the journalist's naïve self-satisfaction, but knew, too, that there was much truth in the little man's boast. Seeing the smile, Mr. Itkin took out his writing pad and his pencil and prepared to make hay while the sun was shining.

It had all been bluff. Mr. Itkin knew no more who those street boys had been than the Procurator himself. But what will not a newspaper man do—or at least promise to do—for ever such a little scoop? But if it had been bluff it had at least been honest bluff, for Mr. Itkin knew how to put himself in the way of getting any information that was going, at least as far as Moscow's night population was concerned. Nor was he disappointed.

On the very evening of the day of his interview with the Procurator—one of those interviews that newspaper men are forbidden to call interviews—he was strolling along the embankment at a sequestered spot when he heard a hoarse whisper from somewhere below his elbow. "Uncle Julius! Eh, Uncle Julius! Gi' us a kopek for a crust of bread, Uncle!"

"Ha! My young friend, Misha!" exclaimed Itkin in delight, wheeling round so as to bring himself face to face with a wizened and undersized morsel of humanity, with a man's leather cap reaching almost to his nose. "The very man I wanted to see! You shall have five griven, if you tell me what I want to know. Which of you boys was it that ran through the yard the night Pavlov was killed?"

One bright eye gleamed up at him rakishly from under the peak of the cap. A skinny hand was held out suggestively.

"A griven for a crust of bread, Uncle!" whined the child.

"Five griven, if you can tell me," maintained the newspaper-man steadily.

"I don't know, Uncle Julius, honest to God, I don't."

"But you can find out."

"I can ask Black-Mug."

"Yes, find Black-Mug. And tell them all there's five griven for anybody who has anything to tell, and Uncle Julius will see that no harm comes to anyone. Here's fifteen kopeks for you now, and the rest when you tell me. Now cut and run. I shall look for you here every night."

Almost before he could turn, the small flying figure was gone at the double, and he waited in vain for its return. He knew enough, however, of the ways of his young friends to feel sure that this was not all he was to hear, and after an hour's stoical pacing up and down the snow-bound streets, he went home, on the whole not unpleased with his first night's progress as a sleuth hound.

The efforts of the State were by the year 1926 causing considerable depletion in the ranks of the flotsam and jetsam of Russian towns, those orphans of the storm, the children set adrift a few years before by famine and civil war, swelling the ranks of juvenile offenders, a menace to the streets at night, and a well-nigh insuperable problem to the educational and municipal authorities. Workshops and clubs were opened all over the towns, homes organised, agricultural colonies formed. Much has been done, culminating in the gigantic effort of the 10th anniversary of the Revolution, during which the streets of Moscow, at any rate, were practically cleared of the savage and pathetic bands formerly infesting them. In 1926, however, the year in which the Pavlov murder was committed, even in the winter, when the waifs were more apt to remain in the Homes, the corners of streets at midnight witnessed many a wild game of cards, the great vats used for boiling tar in mending the roads attracted little gangs of frozen lads, happy to snuggle up under their warm and bulging sides, and even to creep right into them when they had cooled sufficiently. And of a morning the early riser would still meet with a small and tattered rapscallion, his ragged dress crowned by a soldier's khaki helmet on his tousled head, issuing gravely forth from a mysterious doorway in the ancient Chinatown wall, a dented kettle in his hand, on his way to fill it at the half-frozen river, intent and absorbed as any housewife at her morning marketing. Hardly anyone would have had the temerity to follow the young fetcher of water into his den, to penetrate into the group of half frozen youngsters squatting over a fire of sticks on the filthy floor, and even at this early hour deeply absorbed in a greasy pack of cards. At this period the tramway termini were the regular stations of a few young ruffians, who boarded the cars like pirates, seated themselves in a corner and set up a dreary howl intended to be descriptive of their sad fate, to the accompaniment of rhythmic rappings upon their knees with a couple of wooden spoons, loosely tied back to back. With streaming noses, sores on their heads, chilblains on their frozen feet, they overran the streets and markets, the terror of stallholders and street vendors, their pinched faces inspiring the passers-by with fear and pity, their eyes shining with wild emotions unknown to decent citizens.

In the summer their hard lot was somewhat mitigated. They made for the south as regularly as the birds fly north. Every train to the health resorts of the Caucasus and the Crimean coasts bore scores of these passengers on an unwritten free list. Just before the train slowed into any big station a dozen little lads would appear—from between the buffers, from the top of the carriages, from crannies and niches beneath them—each bearing a sack or bag, each with the light of grim determination on his small, harsh-featured face. As soon as the speed of the train allowed, they would drop off the running board and disappear among sidings, trucks, through fields and forests, to frighten the wives of peasants, bask in the southern sunshine, and plunder the countryside of chickens and water-melons.

No one knew the manners and customs of this strange folk better than Julius Cæsarovich Itkin. A subtle sympathy existed between himself and these ruffianly bands. And because he had never once betrayed a malefactor to the authorities—although he had more than once been cognisant of dark deeds and doings—he was trusted as few men of the privileged and sheltered classes are trusted by the outlaws of society. There was a reason for this that was known only to the reporter himself. Not even his friends in the wharves and streets guessed that Julius Cæsarovich Itkin, the best paid reporter in Moscow, had come up to the town himself, fifteen years ago, a ragged and homeless lad, that he too had travelled on trains and under trains, but never in trains, in his wild flight from the small Ukranian town in which his parents, his old grandmother and his two small sisters had all fallen victims to a terrible pogrom. Of those dark and dreadful days he never spoke to any man or any boy, but all their bitterness had been long washed out in a flood of sympathy for small, thieving boys, hungry and cold and homeless, for he never forgot that once upon a time he had himself been just such a small boy.

Itkin knew that all these boys are reckless gamblers and won their hearts by gambling with them equally recklessly. Not that he had brought up from those old hard days any anti-social proclivities, but that he did earnestly desire to understand all the joys and sorrows of his friends, and he knew he could do this better by partaking to them than by standing aloof and offering moral criticism. None of the boys took the trouble to hide their weaknesses from Uncle Julius, who gave a fellow cigarettes, and asked no questions, and therefore it was that Uncle Julius was often in possession of information that the police would have given much to possess, but which they never obtained from him.

Chapter VIII

SILK STOCKINGS DON'T MATTER

TWO DAYS AFTER his interview with Itkin the Procurator received a document through official channels which touched him deeply and made an impression on him which he found difficult to shake off. It was a written statement made by the girl Dolidzey, about whom, by the way, he continued to receive disturbing reports. She was reported to be in a highly nervous condition, eating badly and hardly sleeping at all. Whenever the regulations allowed it she devoured books, of which she received a new one from the prison library almost every day, but otherwise she was listless and apathetic and causing some alarm to the doctor, who feared serious consequences to her health should this deep depression be prolonged. Suddenly, however, she had begged for writing materials and spent hours upon the document which had been delivered into the Procurator's hands at her own request. This document he found to be of such importance that he had it typed to give himself a better opportunity to study it than the scrawled, childish handwriting in prison ink and on prison paper afforded. He took it home with him in the evening and read it and re-read it, each reading convincing him further that the writer was an honest and innocent soul.

"At first I was like a person who has been stunned," wrote Tamara, "I couldn't think, I couldn't reason. It seemed to me as if life had suddenly become cruel and pounced upon me from the shade, like a tiger that had been waiting and waiting. And the most painful thing was to feel that everything was mad, that everything I had up to now believed, was wrong and false and my world had come tumbling down on to my shoulders in little bits. I didn't even think; shall I be punished for something I have or have not done? I didn't even worry about the future. It seemed to me in those awful dark days that I would kill myself if I had to live through them again; that it didn't matter what happened, for the most precious thing in the world that I had always held to like an anchor, had gone from me for ever. And this precious thing was to believe that I could take my life in my own hands, that no one could hurt me so long as I was true to myself, that I was my own best friend and my own worst enemy. How this belief has helped me through hunger and need and through the long, long struggle no one will ever know, and now it had gone, for here was life itself punishing me for something I had never done. That is why I told the Procurator lies at first. I would never have done it if I hadn't been terrified out of my life—not of going to prison or being punished, but because I had lost foothold, for ever it seemed to me. For was it my fault that Pavlov was found stabbed? Why had it to be done with my dagger and at a time when it looked as if I had done it? Is not that sheer wanton cruelty on the part of life? Isn't it stupid, tearing, killing cruelty? So I lied and lied and didn't think what I said. Life was stupid and fate was stupid and so would I be. But worse was to come, much, much, worse. So terrible that I can hardly write it down and must put down my pen to cover my face in agony: after the first two terrible days and nights, a devil seemed to come to me in the night and whisper: 'How do you know you are being punished for what you haven't done? Perhaps you did kill him. You know you meant to. You remember aiming at him with your dagger. Perhaps you really killed him and then went mad and couldn't remember it. Perhaps you are mad now. Perhaps not life is blind and stupid, but you. Just for a few absolutely crazy moments I was glad to think so, for then it would mean that after all I hadn't lost hold on my one principle in life. It would mean that I was only answering for my *actions*. And somehow that didn't seem so bad, and I admitted the awful thought that perhaps it was really I who had killed him and stolen his money, and once I admitted that dreadful idea it haunted me day and night and I thought I should certainly go mad, for underneath, quite, quite, underneath, I knew all the time that I didn't kill him, but it was an agony to cling to that knowledge and often I lost sight of it altogether, and then I felt I was drowning. Again and again I wanted to go to the Procurator and say—'You are right, it was me. I killed him. Punish me and let us finish with it all!' But whenever I got just to this point something kept me back, I suppose the instinct of self-preservation. And then a wild battle between belief and doubt raged for hours and hours and how I ever came out of it alive I cannot tell. All the time the same arguments repeated themselves in my head and went round and round like a round-about: If I didn't do it, then why am I here? Why is life so cruel and so blind? If I did it then it means life is not stupid and blind, but then I am a murderer. I am ruined. I have spoilt my own life at 17. One night I cried and groaned so terribly and uncontrollably that the wardress came in and called the doctor and they were heavenly kind, I shall never forget it, and she gave me something to make me sleep and when I woke up in the morning everything suddenly seemed clear. I knew—but I knew that all the time, of course—that I hadn't done it, but I knew too that I had done something. I had been untrue to myself. And it wasn't life's fault if I got punished for it. And then I could somehow forget about it and I asked for a book from the library and by chance hit upon Tolstoi's *Forged Coupon,* and then everything was blindingly clear—like a flash of lightning. I read that story before and some of the fellows were arguing about it once; they said it was nonsense to argue, bad acts must have a sequence of bad consequences, like in the story, but a good act might have bad consequences and spoil lives, and at the time I thought that a very clever argument. But when I read the story again I knew Tolstoi was right. Bad acts *are* likely to lead to others in a chain, just as it had been with me, only lots of people wouldn't perhaps see what the original bad act had been. Perhaps Tolstoi himself considered it was the forging of the coupon that had been the cause of all the trouble and murders and things, but now I see quite clearly, and I suppose he did too, that the cause of everything was not that, but the unkind illiberality of the boy's father that drove him desperate and made him ready to agree to crime. Yes, yes, that was it. If the boy's father had been more human and decent and given his son two or three rubles to pay his debt, nothing would have happened. And that's just how it has been with me. I didn't kill Pavlov, but it is my fault he died as he did, and not because I went to dance in his room to make a little money, that's nothing, but because I let myself be spoilt by town life and gave in to the general pettiness and vulgarity with which I am surrounded. Pavlov died, not because he had an enemy, but because a foolish girl suddenly felt that she would die if she didn't have a pair of silk stockings. Yes, when Vera came to rehearsal in silk stockings I suddenly felt so miserable and ashamed in my wretched cotton stockings that I decided to agree to go and dance for Pavlov, though I had already refused him three times. I know Vera is unprincipled, I know she hasn't any brains and will never have my technique, and suddenly I felt myself smaller and worse than her, all because she had a miserable pair of silk stockings on, and I who have struggled and fought and bit my way from east to west, I who have meant to dance in the theatre since I was nine years old, I who have lived on buckwheat kasha and black bread without a murmur for years—yes, years—I suddenly felt if I didn't have a pair of silk stockings my life wouldn't be worth living. Oh, Tamara, Tamara, how life has spoilt you, or rather how Moscow has spoilt you. I am almost glad to find myself in prison, if only that I can once again see clearly that SILK STOCKINGS DON'T MATTER—THEY ARE NOT A MATTER OF LIFE AND DEATH. I write this extra big, because it is so important, because a man had to be murdered and I had to be put into prison and goodness knows how many other people had to be frightened and browbeaten, before I could understand this. Oh, that rotten atmosphere of the theatre!

"Now I am ready to tell the Procurator everything as it really happened and it seems to me he must believe it, it seems to me it would be impossible not to believe it, BECAUSE IT IS TRUE, TRUE, TRUE!

"Well, so that wretched Pavlov had been hanging round me for the last six months and bothering me to come and dance for his friends, and praising up my technique and Lord knows what, though I don't believe he has the slightest idea what technique is, and I know for a fact that what he really liked about me was my legs, he told Vera so. After all the only bright spot in this whole wretched affair is that it was Pavlov murdered and not a more useful man. Of course he showed himself in the end to be not at all a bad sort of chap, but life wants more than that of folk nowadays. It isn't enough for me or anyone else to be not bad and kindish and all that. We can even be bad if we like, but we must mean something and mean it hard and all the time, like I meant to dance when I was a little thing of nine in Tiflis. When people mean things as much as all that, they do them. Well, poor Pavlov, I don't believe he ever meant anything except be as comfortable as he could and never miss a ballet, and of course such people don't leave much of a gap behind them. However, that's not what I meant to write. Well, so, as I say, he kept on bothering me and badgering me and the other girls asked me why on earth I didn't go because he would pay me well and I should have a pleasant evening with good things to eat and drink. Yes, of course, I like that, but not among all those foreigners and high-toned people that a man like Pavlov would invite to see a ballet girl dance. If you had only *one* of the lovely things that they give you, to eat off a piece of paper in the wings, it would be a regular holiday, whereas when you get among strangers you can't feel any honest appetite, or if you do you daren't show it, and you keep watching the others to see which fork to take and everything might as well be sawdust. No, thank you, that's a small inducement. Well, so I refused him every time, but as I say one day Vera came to rehearsal in silk stockings and her legs are much worse than mine, but she did look so really elegant and I suddenly felt so terribly shabby and poor, and when Pavlov came round to the wings that night, without thinking at all I agreed to Saturday night after the ballet. So he called for me at the stage door in a taxi and it was the first time I ever had a ride in a car. I was simply longing to ask him to go a long way round, but of course I didn't dare. In about half a minute it seemed to me we got to his house, and I remember so clearly how the car stopped just under a lamp post. Pavlov stood counting his change and a night watchman was standing at the gate and he made me feel not so lonely so I purposely said good-evening to him so as to make myself feel more at home, and he answered me and then Pavlov came after me and helped me through the yard and up the stairs to his room. And then I saw in a minute that there wasn't going to be any company and that everything was prepared for me to be alone with him the whole evening. If I hadn't taken off my clothes in the hall I would have walked straight out, but when I said 'You've brought me here under false pretences,' he came and put his arms round me and what made me see red was that I felt his bad breath puffing up into my face, so I said—'You let me go, you old beast, or it will be the worse for you,' and I struggled to get free. But he only laughed and said what a wild little savage and tried to kiss me. Then I felt my head go round and really scarcely knew for

a minute what I was doing and if I didn't remember so clearly
everything that came after this moment it would be easy for
anyone to persuade me that I had killed him. I got my right
hand free and pulled my dagger out of my belt and I believe
I would have stuck it into him only he caught hold of my wrist
and did something or other with his thumb that made me spread
all my fingers wide and the dagger flew past him out of my
hand. Then he seemed to get quite jolly, all of a sudden, and
let me go.

" 'Come, come,' he said, 'it's not so bad as all that, you know.
You've no need to defend your virginity with a knife, I'm sure
I don't want anything from you that you don't want to give me.
Sit down and let us have a talk. I admire your spirit, I assure
you I do.'

" 'What's the good of talking,' I said. 'You think every ballet
girl must be a prostitute. We shall never understand each other.'

" 'I don't, upon my word, I don't. Tamara, dear, forgive me.
You know you're so confoundedly young and pretty (and I'm not
a bit, I know I'm not—pretty, I mean. Of course, young I am),
that it makes a man's head go round. But I won't come near you
again if you don't want me to. I promise you I won't.'

" 'You may rest assured I don't want you to,' I said, 'and if
you don't mind I'll go home at once.'

"He begged and begged me to at least have a glass of wine
and a sandwich with him to show I had forgiven him, but I
told him I hadn't said a word about forgiveness and all I wanted
was to go home. When he saw I had quite made up my mind he
took out his pocket-book and began hunting through it. I told
him he needn't think of paying me for I didn't take money that
I hadn't earned. He put the pocket-book down, open on the
writing table, and I could see it was stuffed with notes, and turned
round with a note in his hand. 'Look here, kid,' he said, 'how
much do you get at the theatre?' 'I've just begun to get 60
rubles a month since I've been appearing,' I said, 'but that's neither
here nor there.' 'Yes,' he said, 'and if a show you're billed to
dance in is cancelled at the last moment, aren't you paid?' So
I told him of course we get some compensation and the prin-
cipals get the whole fee whether they appear or not, and he said,
well wasn't this just the same thing, for I had given up the time
and counted on the earning and somehow I let myself be per-

suaded into taking the notes he stuffed into my hands. I didn't count them or anything, but when I got into the street I saw there were three for 30 rubles each and one for 10. And I walked home all the way, half disgusted with myself for taking money I hadn't earned, but half the time thinking of the silk stockings I should buy on Monday. And that's all I know about Pavlov's murder. I only remembered my dagger when I was undressing and was vexed that I had given Pavlov another opportunity to see me. I don't know how it came about that he was killed with my knife, but I suppose somebody came in after me and found the dagger by chance. It may have been sticking into something, it was very sharp and very light. I couldn't remember hearing it fall when I thought things over, but I don't know any more.

"The next day (Sunday) somehow I felt a bad taste about the whole thing and I was sorry I'd told the girls I was going because some of the fellows were saying that there had been a row about some of our girls spending the evening and dancing at one of the foreign embassies and they'd been called to the GPU and questioned. Of course a speculator isn't so bad as a military attaché, but still I wished I hadn't had anything to do with it and I no longer cared a bit about the stockings. And so when the Procurator questioned me about the dress and the dagger I thought somebody had told on me and my only thought was to prevent anyone from finding out that I had been there alone and taken money for nothing. And after that I only felt blind panic and fear and simply told one lie after another.

"Now, friend Procurator, you are welcome to believe my story or not, I don't care a pin. I'm not a murderer and I'm not a thief and all the courts in the world can't make me one."

Chapter IX

A LETTER FROM ANON

SOMEHOW THE NOTE of defiance on which the statement ended struck the Procurator as authentic. It moved him as no pleadings, nor the most earnest assurances could have. This plucky little kid, he thought, whether she did it or not, has been accused by society of the capital sin against society—the taking of life. And instead of going under and begging for mercy she shakes her little fists at the agents of the law and says, in effect: "Nothing your clumsy apparatus can do can make me a murderess. I, Tamara, defy you. I am what I am and you cannot change me, though you crush me." Whether murderess or not she was a good plucked one, thought the Procurator.

But however touched he might be by this document, and however privately impressed by its evident sincerity, he could not altogether relinquish the idea of her guilt. The evidence against her was too strong. Pavlov had certainly been killed by her dagger, and she had as certainly been with him within the time when the doctor said he must have been murdered. Moreover she had undoubtedly lied as to her visit to Pavlov, had declared that there had been about fifteen guests, a piano and an accompanist. Might she not be lying now, only more artistically? The Procurator didn't think so, but still . . . that dagger, the hundred rubles in her possession. The Procurator's heart sank as the sense of the black cloud of evidence against the girl overwhelmed him. He could no longer feel impartial; the thought of this young and promising life ruined at its very outset and all for a hundred rubles and a stale sensualist was galling to him. He would have given anything to have his suspicions directed in other channels.

Just when he was beginning to despair of finding any other scent to follow he received a suggestion in the familiar shape of an anonymous letter. There are anonymous letters which sensible men throw straight into the waste-paper basket, and there are others which they study and weigh and ponder over. This one belonged to the latter category. It was from a small town in Eastern Siberia, and was written in an illiterate, almost illegible hand.

I the undersigned have seen photo in police station of A. P. Pavlov, murdered by Caucasian knife in town of Moscow, province of Moscow, and am prepared and ready to swear that I knew subject of said photograph (only he didn't have a beard then, but none the less for that would swear to his eyes at any time, never shall I forget those eyes or evil expression therein) under nomenclature, viz., Malinovsky, when he was head of the notorious White Eagle general staff at Lomsk, during the Kolchak Advance in the year 1919. Was under the impression aforesaid Malinovsky long since gone to his Maker and rendered up his "account" (so to say) but now note he has waited for vengeance to overtake him which he deserved as all who knew him will amply testify but vengeance is mine saith the Lord, I will repay so I take up my pen for purpose of instructing you in my humble opinion this is no mere robbery but political murder from motives of vengeance by one of his countless and numerous victims and I for one though against capital punishment do hereby approve and confirm same."

The signature took two pages, the writer subscribing himself as *A sympathiser with present government, but one who has always kept out of politics and prefers to continue in the same and therefore chooses to remain anonymous so it's no use you trying to trace me for you won't find me besides I have nothing to add though can assure I would if I could.* The Procurator recognised, with a smile, the man who can hardly bear to end a letter, even with his own signature, for the front of the letter was crossed and recrossed with words of approval and mild reproof for "the present government", and stern denunciations of politics in general "which should be did away with if I had my say and will be one day mark my words".

The Procurator found the actual information contained in this letter so important that he took the first opportunity of going with it to the political police—the notorious OGPU—for it referred to the political past of the murdered Pavlov. The writer of the letter had seen a photograph of Pavlov at the local police station, where it had been sent in view of the murdered man's connection with Lomsk, and declared him as a certain Malinosky who had played an important role in Kolchak's army in the 1919 Siberian campaign and had been missing ever since and believed dead.

At the OGPU the Procurator found Tretikov, a man younger than himself by five years or so, but infinitely more crystallised as to his opinions and conclusions. He treated the letter with even greater seriousness than Nikulin privately believed it merited and had before him in an astoundingly short time the full details of the "White Eagle" Society.

"If Pavlov was really Malinovsky," mused Tretikov, "then we've accounted for all but one of that little lot. There were seven of them in all: Bek, Spiridonov and Fedyin we got hold of and know all about their fate; Karavai fell in action, and Volkov died in his bed in 1921, surrounded by his sorrowing relatives. The only ones we never could trace were Malinovsky and a fellow called Milutin. Now supposing Pavlov to have really been Malinovsky, may not Milutin have been his murderer?"

"Motive?" said Nikulin, with raised brows.

"Motive? Well, supposing, for instance, friend Milutin is at the moment occupying an honoured position in some government department! I assure you this is by no means a far-fetched supposition. In that case the only man who could, or would conceivably be likely to denounce him would be Malinovsky, the only one of the band left alive."

"But if Pavlov is Malinovsky, why should he bother to denounce Milutin?"

"No special reason, of course, but the very fact that he could conceivably do so, that he possibly holds some documents, some incriminating photographic group, would give a man trembling for his safety no peace. After all in Pavlov's position he could at any moment go to the States and stay there so that he could denounce Milutin with impunity. He may have found it useful to hold this over Milutin's head, in case of a private quarrel, or a rivalry about some woman—this Dolidzey girl, for instance."

The Procurator shook his head.

"Doesn't seem very likely. His acquaintance with Dolidzey appears to have been very slight, and her only other admirers seem to be the young fellows in the ballet school."

"Well, yes, I merely offer tentative suggestions. But I would be ready to swear that if Milutin knew that Malinovsky was still alive he spent a good part of his waking hours planning to get him put out of the way, and thus the last piece of evidence against himself destroyed. How do we know that documents were not stolen from Malinovsky-Pavlov and the money stolen as a blind? How do we know that Dolidzey's confession is not absolutely true and that, after she left Pavlov, Milutin came in to make an attempt to get the documents, found Pavlov seated at the gramophone and unaware of his entrance, saw the discarded dagger, and felt the opportunity too good a one to miss."

Nikulin was thoughtful.

"The only paper unaccounted for among Pavlov's things is a note signed 'S'," he said. "Supposing, according to your theory, Milutin is alive and in Moscow, and the writer of this note. It is obvious that whoever he was, the writer was on intimate terms with Pavlov, for he addresses him as 'thou' and we have been unable to unearth a single intimate friend of Pavlov so far."

"No one claimed the honour?" said Tretikov, smiling grimly.

"What was Milutin's christian name?" asked the Procurator.

Tretikov shuffled the sheaf of documents before him.

"He was christened Evgeni, Patronymic Antonovich, but that means nothing. Men are always apt to change their names, or at all events adopt a nickname, when they join secret societies, as we have reason to know," smiled Tretikov. "There are sufficiently respectable precedents for *that*. Now about this 'S'—is there anyone among the known acquaintances of Pavlov either whose surname or christian name begins with an 'S'?"

"There is a typist in his office who is called Sophie and a book-keeper called Simyonev, but I have been into their pasts with extreme thoroughness and find everything is known about them. The letter 'S' seems to be leading us down a blind alley."

CHAPTER X

A BREATH OF AIR

A SOUND OF rushing waters came from the drains below the gutters. Pedestrians walked in the middle of the road to avoid the shovelfuls of snow that men on the roofs were casting into the streets. First the snow began to slip from the domes of the churches, so that their blackish gold shone through, then it melted from the grassy slopes under the Kremlin walls, and the grass and the old brick walls looked as if they had been freshly painted from a child's box of paints. Side streets became rushing rivers only to be forded with the help of a bit of short planking, or a large stone or two placed there by thoughtful citizens. The izvoschiks put away their toylike painted sledges, and came out in shabby four-wheeled open landaus, thel left off their shaggy caps and doned curious cylindrical hats with widened crowns and curly brims and a buckle in front. A tender crimson crept into the early sunset, daily growing later, and the cawing of the noisy rooks began to mellow and soften as with great expectations of worms in the turned earth. And then the snow came down thick and fast again, the sledges and sheepskin caps had to be brought out again, and pedestrians and horses slipped about and broke their legs on a surface like glass. And the next day it thawed and everything was to do all over again. This was the supreme moment for citizens to awake to the angry realisation that there were not enough goloshes to be had. The sign over the private bootshops; NO GOLOSHES and the queues outside the government rubber shops are about as reliable signs of spring as can be found. The vendors of coloured stockings hurried their wares out on to the pavements and at every street corner ladies might be seen trying on bust bodices under their loosened coats. Pitiful little bunches of snowdrops and aconites almost smothered in ivy leaves were sold for exorbitant prices and the *Moscow Star* came out with leaders on the probabilities of the river overflowing its banks, and sarcastic poems about the dearth of goloshes and colds in the head. And then suddenly all the pavements were dry and the children covering them with cabalistic signs in white chalk and propelling a potsherd over the signs with the toe of one boot. In fact hop-scotch just as it is played down our alley.

Last of all the ice began to move down the river, and then the hoodie-crows knew spring had really come, and after discussing their plans vociferously for a few evenings from every roof and every tree, going continually and beautifully into perspective and changing their minds and coming back again, they suddenly rushed off one day in a body to the country, and the next day the sparrows had the whole town to themselves, or so they thought.

And the crowds collected on the bridges, so that mounted police had to be employed to keep moving them on, or they might have endangered the safety of the piles, and they surged along the banks for hypnotised hours, staring at the floating ice, coming first slowly, in isolated lumps and at last converting the whole surface of the river into a mass of jostling floes, racing under the bridges and crashing up against their piles, there to be split neatly in two, like giant lumps of sugar, to be caught backwards for a moment by the swirling current, and then impelled forward in midstream, to rush on to the next bridge. Before the last lumps of ice had disappeared, fishermen, as bold now as they had been patient in the winter, were leaving the current in their little boats, and casting nets over the side in scriptural fashion, for the fishes brought down with the swollen waters. Little boys hovered on the brink with little nets and pails; behind them hovered their little sisters with jam jars in which they occasionally received with solemn elation a small brown fish, darting with gasping jaws from side to side of its prison. Next came the boys and girls in boats on the subsiding waters, sculling against the strong currents with bared arms and legs; the first two gulls descended wheeling and screaming over the river, as if they had tumbled down from the very top of the sky and only just stopped themselves from falling into the water. Lilac appeared like a subtle smoke over garden railings. Clouds of dust bowled along the roads like genii from the Arabian nights seeking vengeance on man. The principal roads were closed to traffic one after another, always it seemed at the most inconvenient possible moment, but always to the joy of Mr. Itkin's friends, who tossed their coins in the middle of the Tverskaya, unharried by hoof or wheel, and slept warm at nights against the giant vats. Scaffolding began to appear in the Red Square for May Day celebrations; the streets grew merry with the drums of the pioneers, with flags, with the strains of the International in conflicting keys, and at street corners children bought ice-cream, and parched citizens ordered drinks from coloured syphons. Spring had really come and brought summer along with it, as it does in Russia.

And Tamara, as keenly alive to the changing seasons as a bird, Tamara, who loved to stand on the bridge and gape at the floating ice, who could wait in a golosh queue and scold a shopgirl with the best, who loved to distraction to stand in front of a stall pondering deeply the rival attractions of beige or grey stockings; whose soul loved nothing so much as to march behind a drum and sing the International; Tamara, all of whose spare kopeks went on ice-cream and raspberry lemonade; Tamara to whom the boys brought sixpenny bunches of the first primroses, and sprigs of lilac stolen in quiet squares. . . . Tamara languished in a narrow cell and spent the gladdest time of all the year in the dismal and unaccustomed contemplation of her own soul.

She became so languid and listless that her condition began to cause the prison doctor serious alarm. He saw that this sturdy child of the fiery Caucasus, who could endure hunger and hardship, of whom it was said that at the age of twelve she had danced her way, subsisting on black bread alone, from Tiflis to Moscow, could not bear up against the solitude and oppressive monotony of prison life.

Then it was that one day, after a terrible night spent in sobbing and moaning, she had surprised her warder by asking for writing materials, with which she was immediately and generously supplied by the Procurator's orders. In a day or two this indulgence was rewarded by the production of the document that had so moved the Procurator.

After having read and re-read Tamara's confession the Procurator felt that there were still several points which further conversation with the girl might help to clear up. He therefore sent for her the next day, hoping to find her in a more communicative state of mind than before. The change in her appearance shocked him, but he thought the expression in the dark eyes a little better than before. She seemed weak and was evidently glad of the chair offered her by the Procurator. Her shabby clothes had not been improved by the time spent in prison and there seemed little of the freshness or charm of youth about her. The Procurator found himself wondering what Pavlov could have found in this girl, who had nevertheless proved as fatal to him as if she had been a first-class beauty.

"Well, Tamara," he said kindly, leaning back and regarding her not without sympathy. "Now I'm sure you've made up your mind to tell me all you know about this wretched affair."

"I have written everything," she said.

"You have, I know, but there are a few points still that you may be able to help me clear up," he said.

"Now you say here," he produced Tamara's ill-written, blotchy manuscript in a neat blue jacket, together with a typewritten copy of it, "You say here," he shuffled the pages, "Yes, here it is—'Perhaps you did kill him. You know you meant to.' What did you mean exactly by that?"

"Well, I aimed my dagger at him," she answered readily enough, "you generally mean to kill a person when you do that."

"Oh, well, not always," the Procurator pointed out. "Sometimes one merely means to threaten. Now what do you think you really meant when you pointed your dagger at Pavlov?"

"Well, of course, the chief thing I meant was to make him leave go of me," admitted the girl, "but for the moment I did see red, and thought I might as well kill the worm."

"So you admit you meant to kill him?"

She seemed to think.

"I think if he hadn't caught hold of my wrist I might have killed him."

"Where did you point your dagger?"

"At the base of his throat."

The Procurator referred to the part in his protocol which decribed the clothing in which the murdered man had been discovered. Yes, Pavlov had been wearing a soft collar, through which he had been stabbed.

"So he caught hold of your wrist. And then what happened?"

"He jerked my hand up and the dagger flew over his shoulder."

"Can you describe to me whereabouts in the room you were standing?"

She seemed to ponder.

"Not very far from the door, I think," she answered slowly. "And rather near the writing table it must have been, for I remember he turned me right round after the dagger had fallen and pressed me against the edge of the table for a moment."

"That means that before that *he* must have had his back to the writing table," said the Procurator.

"I suppose so," she said. "Oh, yes, of course, because I could see a little statue of a dancer over his shoulder, and it was standing on the writing table, I know."

"How do you know?" interposed the Procurator quietly.

"Oh, well, I noticed it as soon as I got into the room," she said, "it was the first thing I saw. I suppose being a dancer myself I would notice it."

There was something extraordinarily satisfactory and solid about her replies. And the Procurator knew beyond the shadow of a doubt that she was right. The statuette had been standing on the writing table when he saw the room.

"Well, then, let us proceed to the next point," he said, referring again to the document before him.

Something in his tone seemed to cheer the girl up. It was a certain confidence that all unconsciously was pervading his whole attitude.

"You say that as soon as he had manipulated with his thumb to make you let go of the dagger he got quite jolly all of a sudden and let you go. And yet just now you told me he turned you right round so that he pressed you against the desk. Why did you not write this down?"

"Well, I forgot," she said. "I remembered now, when you asked me how we were standing. He swung me right round, it's true, but when he saw he was pressing me against the desk he let me go."

The Procurator passed on to the next point. It was true, he knew, that two accounts written by the same person of the same event, within twenty-four hours of each other, generally differ in some detail without any conscious dishonesty on the part of the writer, but simply owing to the associations roused at the moment.

"Then the dagger. You didn't hear it fall?"

"No, I didn't," she said with knit brows, evidently perplexed. "I didn't think of it at the time, but afterwards, I remembered that I never heard it fall. I thought I either must have been too upset at the time or it must have stuck into something. It was very sharp, you know."

"And you didn't look for it at once? How was that?"

"I really couldn't tell you. I didn't, that's all. I don't know if I forgot, or what, it must have gone clean out of my head."

"And when did you first remember it?"

"Only when I got home and found I hadn't got it on."

This tallied with the account she had given in the document. Try as he would the Procurator could by no means get her to contradict herself.

"Well, then," he said, "we must suppose, according to your statement, either that the dagger fell on the carpet, in which case it would make no noise in falling, unless it struck against some piece of furniture, or that it stuck into the wall or something and remained there held by its point. Is that possible?"

"Of course it is," said the girl with warmth. "You throw a dagger at the wall and it'll stay there."

"Then we ought to be able to find a mark in something, if this was the case," said the Procurator.

"Of course," she agreed.

He looked across at her. She seemed a different girl. She was still pale and wan, but some fire had crept into her face, and she tossed a heavy lock out of her eyes with an energetic movement of her brown hand that was not without beauty. The Procurator had to reflect, not for the first time, that prison is no beauty cure. Youth seemed to have crept back into the veins of the young creature opposite him, during half an hour in a more normal atmosphere than the solitude of her cell.

He had an idea.

"Now, look here, Tamara," he said. "You know all we want in this case is to discover the truth and the criminal. I don't know if you were the murderer—I don't say you were, I don't say you weren't. But one thing I do know—you can help us to get at the truth, but only by being absolutely frank. I am going to take you to Pavlov's rooms, and you are going to show me to the very best of your ability exactly how you stood in the room when you pointed the dagger at Pavlov."

Her eyes widening in her paling face.

"To Pavlov's room?" she said.

"Yes, to Pavlov's room. No one can show us as well as yourself the exact position you were in and where you stood. Come, Tamara, pull yourself together! If you *didn't* do it, you have everything to gain and nothing to fear from the truth, you know. And if you *did*, then no shrinking from the truth can help you, for we want the truth and we know we shall get it."

She gazed avidly around her in the passage from the door of the police station to the car drawn up at the kerb. The Procurator had often seen the greedy look of the prisoner released for a moment, how he seems to want to lose nothing—not a single item of the clothes of the passers-by, not a shop window, not a dog, or a child. Just before stepping into the car before the Procurator, she looked backwards as if she could not bear so soon to part with the dear street.

"Get in, Tamara," said the Procurator gently.

Seated in the comfortable car, with Yanovitsky on the collapsible seat in front, and an armed man beside the chaffeur, Tamara sank back luxuriously against the cushions and a childish smile lit up her wan features for a moment.

"Why did she smile?" wondered the Procurator, but restrained the question for fear of embarrassing her.

She seemed visibly affected by the short passage through the yard and up the stairs to Pavlov's room, and before the sealed door shrank back piteously for a moment. The Procurator watched her closely—was this the agony of guilty associations or mere natural shrinking from approaching a neighbourhood that had cost her so much grief and pain? Difficult to say.

The room was pretty much as it had been, except that the food had been cleared from the table and the gramophone taken away, reposing at the moment in a locked cupboard in the Procurator's office. The policeman was left outside the door, and the three—the Procurator, Yanovitsky and the shrinking girl, were alone.

"Now, Tamara," said the Procurator, "please stand where you think you were standing when Pavlov took hold of you and tried to kiss you."

She looked round wildly for a moment and then stepped uncertainly on to the edge of the carpet a few paces from the door.

"Here, I think," she said, with a timid glance at the Procurator.

The Procurator stepped over to her side.

"You think you were standing here?" he repeated. "Well, now I'm going to ask Yanovitsky here to come and stand in front of you and hold you for a moment, if you don't mind. And you must pretend to think he is Pavlov. He's not very like, I'm afraid."

The grinning Yanovitsky stepped sheepishly enough to the place indicated and he and Tamara stood for a moment regarding each other stupidly.

"So," said the Procurator, going up to them and walking all around them. "You were so, facing the desk, and you can see this doll-thing here" (the Parisian lady still smiled knowingly from the top of the bureau), "over Yanovitsky's shoulder. Was that just how it was with Pavlov?"

"I think I saw it over his other shoulder," said the girl doubtfully. "I'm not sure, but I have a sort of feeling it was that way."

"Take a step to the left, Yanovitsky," commanded the Procurator.

"Yes, that was it!" exclaimed the girl. "I could just see her head over his right shoulder."

"So that if the dagger flew out of your hand over his shoulder," said the Procurator meditatively, "it must certainly have made a noise falling on the floor, for you are standing on the very edge of the carpet."

They both looked involuntarily towards their feet. Yanovitsky barely touched the carpet with his toes.

"And if," continued the Procurator, "it stuck in something, we've got to find the mark. I want you, Tamara, to go over there and sit down while Yanovitsky and I have a look round for this mark. And I'm going to trust you not to move from your seat till I tell you."

She crossed the room obediently and seated herself on a chair in the opposite corner, watching the movements of the two men eagerly.

The Procurator first went carefully over the surface of the wallpaper, going over every inch of it with his finger tips, while Yanovitsky felt the door and the wainscoting. They were over twenty minutes doing this, during which time the girl at the other end of the room seemed to pass through some deep, absorbing excitement, to a sort of coma. She started violently at the sound of the Procurator's voice.

"So far, nothing," he was saying to Yanovitsky. "Now for the writing table."

Tamara seemed to come to life, and leaning forward again followed the two men with her eyes. Suddenly the Procurator stopped, bent over the desk, straightened up again, and stepped to his attaché case, which he had left on the floor beside the door. Unlocking it, he took from it a small parcel. With bated breath Tamara recognised her dagger. Laying it on the writing table the Procurator first drew from his pocket a small magnifying glass with which he examined, with the utmost attentiveness, something he seemed to have found on the top of the bureau, not far from the feet of the waxen statuette. With a glance backwards, as if to see if Tamara was still sitting in her place, he called to Yanovitsky, who took the magnifying glass from him and also examined the place on the desk. The Procurator then took up the dagger and seemed to be fitting it into something. Tamara almost screamed with anxiety and suspense, when he put away both dagger and magnifying glass without a word.

"Come," he said with sudden briskness, "there's nothing more to be done here. Tamara. Get up."

She rose almost tottering and staggered across the room. She moved her lips but no words came and she could only look her question, with beseeching eyes. He returned her look with pitying comprehension. Then he nodded.

"We found a scar in the wood that might easily have been made by your dagger," he said.

"Oh, God!" she sighed.

Once again in the car the same curious smile flitted for a moment across her wan features. The Procurator felt his curiosity thoroughly roused.

"Why did you smile again?" he said. "When we got in you smiled too. What made you?"

She smiled again and looked at him from candid brown eyes.

"It was one of my silly thoughts made me smile," she said.

"Well, what was it? I don't suppose I should think it silly."

"I was thinking—but you'll think me terribly silly, I'm afraid —I was just thinking how all my life I'd longed to go for a ride in a motor car with lovely cushions and all these looking-glasses and watches and silver things in front, and now here I am and still it doesn't exactly make me happy. I was just thinking that perhaps it isn't always the happiest thing to get the things you wish for. I think I'm rather like the woman who's husband wished the black pudding on the end of her nose."

The naïve avowal left the Procurator profoundly touched. As they drew near the police station Tamara stretched out a timid tentative hand towards her neighbour.

"Have I got to go back there?" she pleaded. "Must I really?"

"I'm afraid you really must," said he, "but cheer up, it may not be for long, you know."

"But you know now that—that I—"

"We know now that you may have been speaking the truth when you say that the dagger flew from your hand and stuck in the wall or somewhere," he said. "But we know nothing more."

"But doesn't that prove that I didn't kill him?" she faltered.

"It proves nothing, my child," he said trying with a touch of sternness to harden his unconscionably softening heart towards this possible murderess.

CHAPTER XI

A BALLET BOY

THE NEXT DAY Yanovitsky had a report to make. A young man was always hanging around the prison where Dolidzey was confined and had twice tried to bribe the officials there: once to get a letter to her, another time to get an interview. He was a tall, slim young fellow, fair and feminine looking, according to the detective's report. "Dubinsky," said the Procurator to himself. The next day he had the young man in question brought to him.

The Procurator felt himself battling with a certain prejudice against the boy. Ballet girls are one thing, he thought to himself, but ballet boys—he shrugged his shoulders and laughed at his prejudice.

The boy was deathly pale, and his hands shook as he answered the questions fired at him one by one.

"When you came to me before," said Nikulin, "as far as I remember, you were suffering from a bad memory."

"Because I didn't want to repeat a lot of silly girls' chatter," muttered the lad.

"You were not asked to repeat anything," said the Procurator quietly. "You were asked if you remembered a certain conversation."

"I was asked if I remembered a lot of silly girls' chatter," said the lad hotly. "And I didn't. I've got more to keep in my head."

"Very good," said the Procurator, "And now what have you got to tell me?"

"Citizen Procurator," said the lad, leaning forward, "She didn't do it! I can tell you that for a fact."

"How do you know?"

"Anybody who knew her knows she was incapable of such a thing," said the lad earnestly.

"Is that why you're so sure she didn't do it? Is that why you can tell me for a fact that she didn't do it?"

"Yes."

"Is that all?"

Silence. The Procurator leaned forward and fixed his kindly short-sighted eyes upon the fair, indeterminate young face.

"Tell me all you know, if you wish to save your friend," he said, with a kind of stern persuasiveness.

Silence once more fell between them. The boy fidgeted with some papers near to his hand on the desk before him. Then he raised his grey eyes with a look of piteous appeal to the Procurator's face.

"I don't know anything," he said simply. "I simply feel—I know—she didn't do it. Everybody knows she didn't do it. You've seen her, you've spoken to her. You must feel sure of that yourself."

"Is that what you came to tell me?"

The grey eyes were suddenly flooded with blue, as if pigmented by emotion.

"I'll tell you," he said, "and if you suspect—misunderstand me, I can't help it. I saw Dolidzey on Sunday night, coming out of Pavlov's house. At least I saw her come through the gate. She stood right under the lamp for a moment, and then turned round. She went down the road with her hands in her pockets, whistling softly and—and—nobody could have looked like that—walked like that—who'd killed a man. She couldn't have, Citizen Procurator. If you'd only seen her yourself, you wouldn't have doubted for a moment."

The Procurator privately thought this highly likely.

"Is this your proof?" he asked, smiling.

"If you'd seen her, it would have been proof enough for you," repeated the boy doggedly.

The Procurator leaned forward abruptly, bringing his face close to the young man's.

"And what were *you* doing there, at that time of night?" he asked.

The boy's face changed, and an expression of fear crossed his features.

"I—I was waiting for Tamara," he said.

"Waiting for Tamara. Did she know you were coming?"

"I told her I should come and fetch her home, and she forbade me to."

"How is it you didn't take her home, then, since you were there?"

"I—I dared not. She told me she would never speak to me again, if I followed her about."

"How is it that the night watchman didn't see you hanging about?"

"I stood on the opposite pavement, in the shadow of a doorway. Nobody saw me. I only wanted to make sure she got home all right."

"And did you?"

"Yes. I walked along on the opposite pavement till she got home."

"Ha! You followed her home. And then what did you do?"

"Then I went home, myself."

"Where do you live?"

"Leontovski Place."

"So. About ten minutes from Little Paul Street."

"Yes. I suppose so. I don't know the exact distance."

"So, you had to come all the way back after you had seen Dolidzey home."

"Yes."

"How did you go? I mean did you walk?"

"I had to, it was too late for a tram."

"And what time did you get home?"

"About a quarter to two, I think."

He had the time quite correct. It ought to have taken him about an hour to cover the distance between his own and Tamara's home on foot. And so, by his own confession Dubinsky had been out between twelve and two and in the neighbourhood of Little Paul Street—just the time when, according to the doctor, the murder must have taken place. Interesting. Very. The Procurator shot an instinctive glance at the hands clasped upon the boy's knee. Long slender fingers, the thumb short, the little finger curved inwards. Had they thrust a dagger in a man's jugular? Here at least was motive for murder. Jealousy all but confessed. A few more questions elicited the fact that Dubinsky had implored Dolidzey not to go to Pavlov, that she had at first laughed at him, and then got angry, and told him not to interfere with her, or it would be the worse for him, as she would never speak to him again if she found him following her about.

"Had you been jealous of her before with anybody?" inquired the Procurator.

"I was always jealous of her with everybody," was the naïve reply.

"But especially with Pavlov."

"I wasn't jealous, I knew she couldn't care for him. But I was afraid he might be an old beast and take advantage of a girl if he got her alone. That's why I waited to see her come out. If she had stayed an hour longer I should have gone in to see what was going on."

"And when you saw her come out what did you think?"

"I was relieved to see her come out so early, looking just like herself, and even whistling."

"What did you expect?"

"I was afraid she might stay a long time, and come out looking upset."

"And what would you have done?"

The boy shrugged his shoulders.

"I didn't think about that. I just wanted to see for myself."

After this the Procurator let him go, with a warning not to hang about the prison any more.

Yanovitsky, set upon the young man's traces, was able to confirm most of his statements. He had left the theatre at eleven-thirty on the night of the murder—that is to say, half an hour before Dolidzey had left with Pavlov in a motor, and had arrived home shortly before two. Nobody seemed to know where he had been in the interval, and his own statement that he had hung about watching the gate in Little Paul Street was quite likely to be the true one.

The Procurator felt bound to consider Dubinsky as a possible accessory to the murder. The motive was there, the time coincided. There was the money. Dubinsky had certainly not gone to Pavlov's rooms primarily to steal, but having been there he might have espied the pocket-book on the table, and yielded to temptation, or he might have purposely taken the money to make it look like a murder for robbery. The Procurator played with the idea of arresting the lad, and then renounced it in favour of having him closely watched. Fresh questioning of Tamara's friends in the ballet school evoked the information that Dubinsky's unsuccessful courtship of Tamara was common knowledge—

indeed, almost a common joke—and that Tamara had complained to her friends that she couldn't stand the way Dubinsky hung about her and spied on her goings in and comings out.

All Yanovitsky's information had been gathered from Dubinsky's colleagues at the ballet school. He admitted having been unable to see the young man's landlady, but believed she would have nothing to add to the information he had collected.

"How was it you didn't see the woman for yourself?" asked the Procurator sharply. "She may prove a most important witness."

"She was always out shopping, or getting herself enrolled as unemployed on the Labour Exchange," said Yanovitsky resentfully. "And she appears to be a perfectly respectable woman. She certainly has nothing to do with the murder."

"Who said she had, fool?" said Nikulin to himself. Aloud he said, "Unemployed, you say? What profession?"

"Bookkeeper. Unemployed eight years."

"Married?"

"Yes. Husband also a bookkeeper. Unemployed nine years."

"How do they live?"

"They don't—at least not to notice. This boy Dubinsky rents their bath-room."

"What does he pay?"

"I don't think he does. Supposed to pay four rubles a month, but the neighbours say he's in perpetual arrears."

"Bring her here—the landlady, I mean," said Nikulin, and Yanovitsky left, with a shrug of his shoulders to carry out what he considered unreasonable instructions.

He was, however, extremely crestfallen when the interview with the landlady was actually what led to the arrest of Dubinsky.

She turned out to be a pinched and shabby young woman with a hopeless expression in her pale blue eyes. Questioned by the Procurator, she said that Dubinsky had been living in her bath-room (which apparently had never within her memory been expected to fulfil its true office) for nearly two years and that he paid her four rubles a month for the privilege.

"You mean he owes it," interpolated the Procurator.

A faint smile on the wan face.

"He generally pays in the end," she said as if apologetically.

"He's a good boy. As soon as he gets the money from his uncle he pays me. Sometimes his uncle isn't very regular either."

"Where does his uncle live?"

"In Kiev."

"When did he last pay you?"

"Monday, February the fifteenth. I looked it up before I came here."

Nikulin glanced up and looking down again made a hurried note.

"And up till then for how long had he owed you?"

"For six months."

"So he paid you twenty-four rubles."

"Thirty, sir. He said he might as well make it a round sum and throw in four rubles, after owing me for so long."

"So-o-o. Has he ever paid in advance before?"

"No, I don't remember that he has. But he's only been with me just two years and he's never left the rent unpaid so long before."

"Do you know why he left it so long this time?"

"I think his uncle missed paying once and that put him out."

After this Dubinsky had to be called again. His sensitive young face showed distinct signs of agitation and he answered the Procurator's questions with obvious nervousness.

"You paid your landlady for six months' rent, and a month in advance and four rubles on Monday, February the fifteenth," said Nikulin in his suavest manner. "Where did you get this money from?"

"I get money from an uncle in Kiev," said the lad.

"Ah, yes, and when did you last get a sum of money from him?"

"I forget."

"Try to remember."

"Over a month ago. Just before I paid my rent it would be."

"How long is it since he sent you a previous sum?"

"About six months."

"Ha! But you don't remember exactly when the long-awaited sum arrived on Monday. Well, about when was it? Before or after noon?"

"Before."

"And when did you pay your landlady?"

"In the evening."

"Why not at once?"

"She wasn't in when the postman came and then I myself went out."

"The money came by post?"

"Yes."

"That means there must be a record at the local post office?"

"I don't know. I suppose so."

"Yes, yes, that is decidedly to be supposed. But we will make sure. Yanovitsky, my friend, you know the district post office for Leontovski Place. You will perhaps have a look for Citizen Dubinsky's receipt for—how much money did your uncle send you?"

"A hundred rubles," muttered the boy. "But I don't remember signing any receipt."

"It is usual to do so when receiving money through the post office," said Nikulin briefly. "But your memory may be at fault."

Yanovitsky was gone three quarters of an hour, during which Nikulin kept the wretched Dubinsky inactive on a bench, while he occupied himself with his papers, keeping the lad, however, under constant observation. One conclusion to which this observation brought him was suddenly to open his cigarette case and pass it over to his victim, who grabbed feverishly at a cigarette and lit up with a mute glance of gratitude.

Yanovitsky returned and said a few words in a low voice to Nikulin. Looking from face to face the anguished boy saw Nikulin's eyeballs roll suddenly from side to side and then remain very steady at some information which his subaltern had just given him. He then turned immediately to Dubinsky.

"The post office has no record of any money received by you on Monday, February the fifteenth," he said. "But it has just received a money order for you from Kiev this evening. You will go with Inspector Yanovitsky to receive this money and come back to me with it, for it will be necessary for me to have an account of it from you."

The two disappeared and were back again within half an hour, Yanovitsky with a sealed envelope in his hand, and a small wad of paper-money.

"Gave it up to me unopened," said the worthy man to his superior and handed both packets across the writing desk himself.

Nikulin passed it back to the young man.

"It's addressed to you. Open it," he said.

Dubinsky took it with a shaking hand, and ran his fingers under the gummed flap. He seemed to read it without understanding it, and handed it back mutely to the Procurator.

My dear nephew, read the Procurator, deciphering not without difficulty the crabbed characters in faint ink. *I have been ill and in the hospital for three months and so could not send you your money. I thought I should never come out of the hospital alive and I didn't want to send you the money in case your aunt wanted it for my burying. Now I am back home again and it looks as if I wasn't going to die this time, so I hasten to send you a 100 rubles, although you must forgive me if I am quite unable to pay up for the last three months and have no prospects of doing so, for things are very bad in my line here and your cousin is going to be married. But I hope you will be soon in a way to earning yourself soon, as you always said you would be able to when you were seventeen, though I never could believe in dancing as a profession for a grown man, but now you are spoilt for anything else, I suppose, and will never be good for honest work again . . .*

More followed in the same grudging spirit, but the only detail of interest was the mention of 100 rubles being transmitted through the post office simultaneously with the letter. After this the arrest of Dubinsky was a foregone conclusion. It seemed to the Procurator that the young man even seemed relieved and lost some of his nervousness. He had often before noticed the soothing effect on a man of being finally pinned down, and at last robbed temporarily of suspense.

Left to himself Nikulin gazed at the incriminating letter, and meditated not for the first time on the seeming malice of Fate. If the cross old uncle had sent this letter earlier no suspicion could have fallen upon Dubinsky, who would have been able quite successfully to account for the thirty rubles he had paid to his landlady. It had come as it was in the nick of time to incriminate him. If Dubinsky had restrained his generous impulse to pay his landlady at once, or his uncle obeyed the impulse to send his nephew money without delay, the boy would not have been under arrest for robbery and murder.

With regard to the money with which Dubinsky had paid his rent he now remained obstinately silent, only denying that he had taken it from Pavlov's rooms, or that he had ever been in them.

"It's no use, Procurator," he said, after a long and exhaustive cross-examination. "I can't just now account for the money, but it wasn't stolen."

"Awkward for you," said Nikulin.

"All right. It *is* awkward, I admit, but truth will out. I never killed a man or stole a kopek."

"And you have nothing more to tell me?"

The lad was silent.

"When are you going to let Dolidzey go?"

"Why should we let her go at all, since we've got her?" asked Nikulin quizzically.

"What's the good of keeping us both? We can't both of us have done it?"

"But that's just what you may have done. How am I to know that you're not accomplices?"

The boy raised startled grey eyes.

"Accomplices!" he exclaimed, and it seemed to Nikulin that the very idea startled him. "You know perfectly well we're not."

"I know nothing of the sort," returned Nikulin, "and until you can prove that you are not, I am well within my rights in retaining you both."

CHAPTER XII

HONOUR AMONG THIEVES

MR. ITKIN HAD known where to put himself in the way of hearing more from his young friends about the Pavlov murder. But he was doomed to disappointment, for it was more than two weeks before he could come across anyone who could enlighten him in regard to this affair. Spring had gone back on her promise in a veritable blizzard, and here was April wearing the face of January, before he again heard the whisper: "Uncle Julius! Hey, Uncle Julius!" This time he was sharp enough to catch the whisperer by a lean elbow, and turning, found himself looking down into a pair of blue eyes gleaming from under a tattered soldier's cap with ear-flaps.

"Ha! My young friend Misha!" he exclaimed. "You were in such a hurry when last we met that you couldn't stop to have a little chat. I hope you have more time at your disposal now."

The boy grinned, his small, twinkling eyes rolling rapidly from side to side.

"Come on!" he said, "the air's not healthy here to-night."

He glanced nervously at the back of a policeman, and Itkin without a word turned and followed him.

The boy led the way down towards the river. Like the great wall of the Kremlin, that of Moscow's Chinatown is flanked with round bastions, and it was towards one of these that the boy led his companion. He pushed in a low, ramshackle door with a careless shove, and they both entered. It was icy cold inside the tower, little warmer than on the frozen street, but this did not prevent it from being both close and frowzy. A lantern hung from a nail on the brick wall, shedding its pale beams on a sight that would have surprised any but Julius Cæsarovich Itkin. Four boys sat cross-legged on a piece of tarpaulin on the earth floor, throwing down flaccid cards on to an upturned bag in the centre, in the middle of which was a heap of small coin, dirty scraps of paper, and buttons. Behind them, seated on packing cases, bricks and stones, crowded five more boys. All followed the game in absorbed silence, only looking up for a moment at the entrance of Itkin and his guide. There were boys of all ages and a couple of young fellows, who might have been over twenty. All the faces were reckless, pinched, and old-looking; all had reddened noses. Some wore dilapidated padded coats and sheepskin caps, some were shivering in rags through which a sharp elbow protruded, some had a man's overcoat held across their meagre chests with a safety-pin. Most were smoking, and all were perpetually spitting. Itkin lit a cigarette and passed his silver case from hand to hand. Every boy took one, and when one of the over-grown youths took three, there were ready hands to remove the two he had placed behind his ears and return them to the case. When the case got back to Itkin he quietly put it down, open, on the corner of the card table, and waited in silence for the game to be over. No sound but an occasional expectoration, a hollow cough and stentorious breathing interrupted the calls of the players, when suddenly one of the boys flung down his hand and flew at the throat of the boy opposite. Instantly the table was kicked over, cards, coins and cigarettes flying in all directions, the air was filled with oaths and cries, and the two boys lay on the ground, their respective supporters falling over each other, and coming to blows among themselves. Mr. Itkin sat calmly smoking and waiting for the fracas to be over, which it was as suddenly as it began, leaving behind it nothing but a bruise or two, a little blood from a couple of noses, and a few very rude words. Some-one had been discovered cheating. The table was righted, the cards gathered up, the coins and paper groped for. Money and I.O.U.'s were scrupulously returned to their former owners, the cheating having neutralised all winnings. Only the silver cigarette case did not reappear, but its owner seemed to have forgotten all about it. The cardsharper, a heavy overgrown lout of seventeen, was bundled ignominiously away, and the door pushed to again by the nearest foot.

"Shall I take a hand, boys?" offered Mr. Itkin, and the cry went eerily round the weird cave: "Uncle Julius! Uncle Julius is going to play!"

Just as the game was beginning, the boy Misha, who had been squatting on his heels against the wall, suddenly started to his feet, and ran like a hare to the door. As it banged to behind him the newspaper man looked round anxiously.

"Where's Misha off to?" he said. "I want him. Fetch him back somebody."

"He'll be back soon," said someone easily. "I expect he's gone after your cigarette case."

"Oh, is that all?" said Itkin, reassured, and turned his whole attention to the game.

In ten minutes the boy Misha was back again, breathless.

"Here you are, Uncle," he said, holding out the silver case. "Who brought that thief and cardsharper here?"

Itkin understood perfectly that the moral indignation, sincerely shared by all, was directed not against thieving and cardsharping, but against robbing and cheating one's own set. After the game at which Itkin, in spite of his honest efforts to cope with his opponents, lost three rubles, the boys crowded round for "a story", to which they listened with the eager absorption of children pushing off the bedtime hour. Itkin had provided himself with a tattered copy of Jules Verne and read till his throat ached. When he had finished and satisfied various eager questions and comments, he said, putting the book away in his pocket: "Now, boys, who killed Pavlov?"

There was a moment's silence, some subdued chuckles, a good-humoured oath, and a shrill voice from the back of the cave-like room cried: "That's not what Uncle Julius came for to-night! Yes, I don't think! He just came to read a pretty story to his dear little boys."

The sally was greeted with general laughter, and when it had died down Itkin repeated his question. This time it was answered by silence only. He turned to Misha, but Misha seemed to have disappeared as if by magic.

"Look here, Uncle," said a stunted lad with hard features, but honest-looking brown eyes. "It wasn't any of the boys."

"I know it wasn't," said Itkin, "but it wasn't a girl, either."

This tickled their fancy, and the gloomy cave again rang with hoarse laughter.

"And another thing," continued the lad who had first spoken, "there's not one of us boys here can tell you. Only Black-Mug Peter knows."

"Well, that's just what I thought myself," said Itkin, looking round, "but I expected to find Peter here. Where is he?"

"Peter's gone to by-byes," cried a voice. "It's time for little boys to be in bed."

"Black-Mug's nabbed," said a quiet voice from the crowd.

"When?"

"Last week. Sent straight off to the Labour Colony without a trial. The cop told him last time he was nabbed he'd go straight there and stay till they let him out, if he ever got him on his books again."

"What was he nabbed for?"

"Stealing apples off a store," cried someone amid another gust of laughter, and Itkin understood they didn't mean to tell him.

"And you don't any of you know who killed Pavlov, really?" he asked, for the last time.

"We don't, Uncle Julius, word of honour we don't."

It was not the first time he had believed their word of honour.

The next morning early he set out for the Labour Colony. He knew how the boys dreaded to be sent there—worse than to prison, strange to say, although there was much—an outsider would have said everything—in the régime to make it compare favourably with a prison. Many of the boys in the Labour Colony earned good money in the carpentry and lens-making shops; games, kino-shows and other entertainments were arranged for them; the better-behaved elements were let out on parole during holidays and sometimes on Sundays; and yet most delinquents preferred a sentence in prison, the explanation being that sentences in prison have a definite term and in the case of juvenile offenders are not likely to be very long, whereas in the Labour Colony you stayed until you showed signs of mending your ways and had become an efficient worker in one of the shops. Besides there was the hated three hours' schooling, the perpetual medical examinations, the obligations to work in the shops four hours a day.

The Labour Colony was housed in an unfriendly red-brick building on the outskirts of the town. Nearby, straddled the "Big Kommintern" (the Moscow Radio Station), a vast, light structure, rather like an articulated insect's body. Formerly the house had been a kind of Moscow Marshalsea for merchant debtors. Then juvenile delinquents—hard cases only—were lodged there. Itkin was at home in these precincts, and although the sentry at the gate did not recognise Mr. Itkin, everyone else whom he met did. He made his way easily to the director of the place, who was seated at his desk, with the telephone receiver to his ear, when Itkin entered. The tiny office was crowded up by five boys in dark, crumpled suits, huddled together by the wall, with downcast, discontented faces. Itkin swept a glance over them —Black-Mug was not among them, nor any other of his acquaintances.

"Hullo, Julius Cæsarovich!" cried the Director, "come to visit one of your friends?"

"That's right," said Itkin. "I hear you have my old friend Peter Black-Mug at last."

"Yes, we've got him now, and we're going to keep him till we've done with him," replied the young man. "But have you come to visit him? We'd rather you didn't, you know, in the first fortnight."

"Well, this isn't quite an ordinary affair. I'd rather like to have a talk with you in private."

He glanced at the sullen group in the corner. The director followed the line of his glance.

"Look here, you fellows," he said. "If you've got anything to tell me, I can perhaps give you five minutes now."

There was a stir in the group, someone muttered, but no one said an articulate word.

"You see these chaps don't want to work," explained the Director. "They don't say *why* they don't want to, they just won't, and that's all. And as they have plenty of time on their hands and I didn't know when I should have a minute to spare for them, I thought they might as well cool their heels in here for a bit. They were here three hours yesterday, and they've already been two hours to-day, but as they don't want to work, of course that doesn't matter to them."

"Come on, now, speak up, one of you!" he said, addressing the group in tones of rough familiarity. "We know you don't want to work, but we don't know why? Suppose you tell us."

"We don't want to work for money we never see," muttered one lad, instinctively taking a step forward.

"Aha, that's a reason, now," said the Director. "Any more?"

The other boys nudged the spokesman, who had retreated into the group. He again took a half step forward.

"Why shouldn't we smoke in the shops same as the others?"

"Now you're talking!" said the Director, "and when people talk they can be answered. Now as to not seeing your money, that's perfectly true. But you're fools if you think that makes any difference to you. You can buy what you like through the co-operative."

"There's nothing we want in the co-operative," came a voice from the corner.

"If that's so, then again you're fools," came the inexorable reply. "Who chooses what's to be in the co-operative? I don't you do yourselves. Complain to your co-operative commission, get on to the co-operative commission yourselves. You can order anything you like."

"Vodka?" came a derisive voice and "Snow?" came another.

"Except alcohol or snow, as you are very well aware," said the young Director calmly. "Now as to smoking: in the lens shops, where more metal than wood is used, smoking is allowed. In the carpentry shops, where more wood than metal is used, smoking is forbidden. Before you can be moved to the lens shops you must pass a month in the carpentry shops, so the sooner you get it over the quicker you can smoke at your work. And now if there's nothing else, off with you to the yard, and tell Fedor to give you skates. To-morrow you can tell me whether you've made up your minds to work."

Itkin noticed a gleam come into the dull eyes at the suggestion of skating, but a mutter was heard to the effect that all the skates were blunt, and the ice unfit for use, as the lads shuffled out, some with shamefaced smiles, some with hangdog looks.

"Wait!" exclaimed the Director, holding out a box of cheap cigarettes. "Take these if you prefer presents to what you earn yourselves."

A freckled lad with a snub nose spreading over his flat cheeks suddenly turned at the door, holding up the dingy cavalcade. A very sweet smile lit up his plain face. He put out his hand for the box.

"It's hard for us to refuse cigarettes, Citizen Director," he said. "You know what we boys are. You take everything from us that we love here, and if we couldn't have a fag or two a day, we couldn't stand it. We'll take your cigarettes, but we'll soon return them with our own earnings, won't we, fellows?"

An astonishing change came over the whole group, suddenly as if by magic transformed from a set of half-defective looking criminal types to so many well-liking, jolly lads.

"Yes, Citizen Director! We will! That we will! We'll start in the shops to-morrow!"

"No, to-day! We'll begin to-day!" came other voices.

"All right, lads, you do," said the young man, with a friendly smile, but careful not to show the least hint of triumph at his victory. "I advise you to go off to the rink just now, and to-morrow you can start in the shops from the morning. And then you'll soon be treating me to a box of the best."

"And they will, too," he said, half to himself, half to his visitor, as the door banged behind the eager group.

"You're the lad!" cried Itkin in genuine admiration. "You know those boys, by God! Fancy a box of cigarettes transforming them like that. But of course it wasn't the cigarettes, it was the one touch of nature that got them."

"That's it," agreed the young man. "And once again the filthy and degrading habit of smoking is justified of all its children."

"Still, one feels a bit surprised the first time one sees the boys smoking all over the place," said Itkin. "Most people would expect you to try and break them of it."

"Impossible," said the Director. "We can't break ourselves of it, how can we expect to break these poor lads? We ourselves may be convinced of the harm it does us, and yet we can't stop. And we can never hope to convince them of smoking doing them any harm, they would regard prohibition as mere senseless tyranny, and part of the general conspiracy to rob them of all their joys. You heard what that lad said: 'You take away from us everything that we love,' and of course he's right. We take from them all the joys of the streets. We take them from drink, cards, cocaine, and God knows what other wild pleasures—all the excitement and colour of the streets—we must leave them something to soften the harsh discipline. We must let them see that we are human beings. Besides we couldn't enforce it. If we were to forbid them to smoke we should only have them smoking in secret places and setting the bedclothes on fire. As it is, it is a comparatively easy matter to prevent smoking in dormitories and even confiscate smokes if anyone is caught doing so."

"You're a great lad," said Itkin, "and as for your boys, I love them all, as you know. One day I shall have to leave the paper and come and work with you, I know I shall. Only it would be just as difficult for me to leave the streets as it is for the boys. And now will you let me have a word or two with Mr. Peter Black-Mug? He may be able to clear up a little matter of a murder, if I'm not mistaken."

The Director pressed a bell and sent the man who answered it for the celebrated Peter.

It was a dreadful fellow who arrived in the room, with cropped, pointed skull, flattened nose, and drooping underlip, but Itkin greeted him like an old friend.

"Hullo, Blackmug," he cried, "so they've got you at last, old pal! Ah, Peter, Peter, they must have got up early to catch an old bird like you."

A gratified smile flitted over the fierce countenance.

"Peter's all right," said the Director, "he's already had a fight with the Instructor in the carpentry shop, and made it up, and got promoted to the lens shop in two days. Peter's rapidly becoming a capitalist."

Again a smile of infinite cunning lit up the darkened face.

"Look here, Peter, old man," said Itkin confidentially. "Who killed Pavlov?"

Peter laughed outright, a hoarse, chuckling laugh that seemed to express at least as much malevolence as amusement.

"Well, it wasn't Peter, we know," said the Director, "for he was nabbed on Sunday morning, without a kopek on him. Indeed, we got him in a state of collapse from hunger, trying to break into a grocer's store, didn't we, Peter? And he's been eating like a wolf ever since. And we can't help feeling that if he had had Pavlov's money he'd have treated himself to a blow-out at the Grand Hotel, instead of trying to get into a grub shop by the back entrance. For after all our Peter isn't such a fool as he looks."

Every testimony to his cunning or villainy seemed to delight Peter hugely, and by now he was grinning from ear to ear.

"But who was it, Peter?" asked Itkin, "for we don't believe it was Tamara."

"It wasn't either," said the boy. "But I don't know who it was, all the same."

"Oh, go on, Peter, who knows, if *you* don't?" coaxed Itkin. "I'm sure if they had you in the Police Force you could tell them who did half the murders in Moscow. The other half you wouldn't tell, of course, because they would be your own."

Peter was a veritable prima donna for sweet flattery of this description. He couldn't get enough of it. But nothing could be got out of him. He didn't know who killed Pavlov, honest to God he didn't.

"Then how is it you're so sure it wasn't Tamara?"

"She never done it," said Peter, suddenly earnest.

"Well, you can at least tell me how you know that."

"I can't tell you unless Slippery agrees. You'll have to ask Slippery."

Itkin raised his hands in despair.

"Misha took me to Vanya," he said, "Vanya sent me to you and now you send me to Slippery. And Slippery will send me to some other young ruffian, I suppose."

"Because we all have to give our consent," said Peter gravely, a strange look of dignity ennobling his degraded features.

"So how can I get Slippery to tell me anything either."

"He will, if you take a letter from me," said Peter.

"Give me a letter then, Peter, there's a dear fellow," said Itkin eagerly.

"All right. Better give me some of the Colony notepaper, then he'll be sure it's from me. All the fellows know I've been nabbed," he added with ludicrous grandeur.

It was a grotesque sight to see this clumsy creature labouring with the scratchy pen and thick, violet ink. His tongue hung out like a child of six forming his first pothook; he scratched and scratched at the paper, with his head on one side, till he had filled the whole of one sheet. Then he handed it up to Itkin, who took it with gratitude and respect.

"Now, where am I to find Slippery?" he asked.

Peter considered.

"Very like he'll be working the Stone Bridge this week," he said at last.

On his way home Itkin examined the document. Through blots

and scratches he read: *You can tell Uncle Julius, bearer of same, how we know she never did Pavlov in signed peter blackmug his mark.*

At about midnight of the same day Itkin strolled slowly towards the river. Peter was right—Slippery was "working" the Stone Bridge. Itkin stood against the parapet and watched the process. The boy was standing in his rags and felt boots at a corner of the bridge, spitting out the husks of sunflower seeds, and exchanging badinage with a couple of grown-up loafers, but ever keeping a watchful eye for the approach of a sledge. Traffic over the bridges is only allowed at a foot pace, and this rule is strictly adhered to by the Moscow izvoschiks and insisted upon by the police even at midnight and after, when the only traffic is an occasional light sledge. This strict observance of the law is for once in favour of the street boys. A gay young spark escorting his lady home may prefer to throw out ten kopeks, to being accompanied at a foot pace over the bridge by a running comment on his past, the number of his illegitimate children, and unflattering suggestions as to his race and social origin. As soon as a horse's hoofs touched the bridge Slippery was alongside with a piteous wail, and appeals to the kind and handsome and undoubtedly wealthy and noble "uncle". For about half the length of the bridge he kept this up, but if his pathetic appeals produced no coin, the whining changed to a volley of the foulest abuse and language.

After watching Slippery with admiration for about ten minutes, Itkin approached him and made himself known. He easily persuaded the boy to come with him to a less exposed place, by offering to make good any losses he might be supposed to suffer from abandoning his beat. Slippery led the way towards the vast cathedral of the Redeemer, a huge modern copy of the ancient domes, sheathed in white marble, topped by heavy gilded cupolas, its somewhat pretentious importance still further enhanced by flights of stone steps and terraces all round. The boy, followed by the man, turned to the right, to the tiny red church, one of those that the flames "forgot somehow" when Napoleon set Moscow alight. The little old stone staircase that leads up one side and down the other forms a shelter for many a young miscreant. As Itkin and his guide approached, a bottle flew out, narrowly missing Itkin's shoulder.

"Shut up, you fool, can't you," said Slippery fiercely, running on in front. "Can't you see it's Uncle Julius?"

"Oh, Uncle Julius!" came in a drawl from under the staircase, and a shaggy head peeped out. "I beg your pardon, Uncle Julius, I'm sure. I was just practising to keep my hand in. And I thought to myself—'Here comes a fat speculator, might as well take a shy at him for luck.'"

"Well, then, you're a fool, Fatty, and just shouldn't think, that's all," said Slippery calmly. "Look here, you fathead, me and Uncle Julius have a little private business, so I've left the bridge. Want to go and work it for me? Halves of course."

"All right," said Fatty laconically, creeping out from under the staircase, and starting off at a light, wolf-like run for the bridge.

"Look here, my boy, you don't expect me to get under that staircase, I hope," said Itkin to Slippery.

"No, you're a bit too gigantic for that, perhaps," said the boy ironically. "Come on round the corner, what is it you want?"

Itkin handed over Peter's note in silence. Slippery took almost as long to read it as Peter had taken to write it. Then he handed it back to Itkin.

"That's right," he said, hitching back his sheepskin cap the better to scratch at his scalp. "That's Black-Mug's moniker all right. I knew they nabbed him."

"Well," said Itkin eagerly. "Now, Slippery, are you going to tell me who killed Pavlov?"

"We don't know that," said the boy cautiously. "We only know it wasn't Tamara. That's all we know."

"And how do you know that?"

"And I can't tell you that unless Squinty agrees."

Itkin felt a strong impulse to seize the boy by his frail shoulders and shake him till his teeth rattled.

"You boys will drive me mad," he exclaimed. "I've already been sent from Misha to Vanya, from Vanya to Peter, from Peter to you, and now you want to send me to Squinty. And God alone knows who Squinty will send me to. I wonder what you think you're playing at, all of you. Cobbler, cobbler, mend my shoe, is it? Why, it's as bad as trying to get an answer out of an inquiry to a government office."

"No," said the boy gravely. "If Squinty agrees and me and

Peter agrees, you'll be all right. It's only us three knows and none of us can't tell without the others agree, too."

Itkin groaned.

"Then how in the world am I to find Squinty?" he asked.

"You'll find Squinty," said Slippery reflectively, "you'll find Squinty to-morrow at twelve near the Sukharevsky Tower. There's a boy coming from Tver that plays the concertina a treat, and some of us lads will be there."

"Will you be there?"

"Well, no," he said regretfully. "You see, I'm working the Stone Bridge this week, and it won't do to leave it to Fatty. I'm working it for another fellow what's in trouble, and Fatty isn't so experienced as what I am."

"So you only get half of the half Fatty is getting now?"

"That's right. I get half, and I shall have to give Fatty half of my half to-night for obliging me."

"Never mind that, Slippery," said Itkin, benevolently, "I'll make it worth your while. You know you can trust me. I've never gone back on any of you yet."

"It isn't that, Uncle Julius," said the boy, "it isn't only the money. It's neglecting the work. If I can't get Fatty to take it on again we shall have a boy from another set taking it away from us and a lot of trouble working it up again."

He spoke like a doctor wondering if he could leave his practice for a month.

"But Squinty doesn't know me," wailed Itkin. "He'll never trust a stranger. I don't even know him by sight."

"Anyone'll show you Squinty," said the boy comfortingly. "And there's sure to be some of our lot there that'll know you, Uncle Julius."

"Still, you'd better at least give me your moniker," insisted Itkin. "Come on in here and I'll stand you a beer and a sandwich, and you can write a few lines to Squinty."

The strange couple entered a low eating-house to make the transaction. While beer and a ham sandwich were being fetched the boy embarked upon his message to Squinty, on a piece of paper which Itkin tore from his notebook.

"You give this to Squinty and he'll come," he said reassuringly. "I shall be working the bridge up till about two."

All efforts to buy the boy off being vain, Itkin had to content himself with this second document, and retired to bed for the night.

He had little difficulty on the succeeding night in finding the group of enthusiasts around the concertina virtuoso. It was not, however, so easy to introduce himself into their midst. It so happened that the group contained not a single face that was familiar to him, and he felt himself to be the recipient of black, suspicious looks. Indeed very soon after he came up to them the music ceased abruptly.

"Go on, boys," said Itkin, handing round a box of cigarettes. "I only want to listen, too. I shan't disturb you."

But suspicion was not so easily lulled, and the player could not be persuaded to resume. A small boy in the group suddenly butted at Itkin from the right, but the journalist understood the manœuvre and turned instantly to protect his left, catching a skinny hand just about to investigate the contents of his pocket.

"Is that all you know?" he said good-humouredly. "You think I'm very green—just up from the country, eh?"

The laugh that never failed to greet any attempt at humour arose in the group.

"Where's Squinty?" said Itkin. "I want to speak to Squinty."

Silence and a renewal of the dark, suspicious looks.

"Don't be fools. It's nothing to do with *them*. I have business with him. Slippery sent me to him."

Sullen murmurs broke the heavy silence.

"If I show you Black-Mug's and Slippery's monikers, will you believe me?"

The boys crowded nearer curiously, trying to snatch the pieces of paper from his hand.

"No, you don't," he said, holding them high above his head. "I'll show them to you one by one, if you like, but I'm not going to part with them. This is Black-Mug's—I went to the Labour Colony to get it, and this is Slippery's, he gave it to me last night. He's working the Stone Bridge, that's why he couldn't come here to-night."

He felt he had made an impression. There was some more murmuring and an overgrown boy was pushed forward whom Itkin supposed, from a violent cast in one of his small black eyes, to be Squinty. This boy inspected the two documents with the minutest care, turning them over, reading and re-reading them, and even taking a sniff at them, as if desirous of putting them to every possible test. Then he turned his squinting gaze upon Itkin, took off his cap, scratched his head; replaced his cap, hitched up his trousers, scratched his side, and settled the trousers again.

"All right, I'll come for a whole one." (A ruble.)

"A half (fifty kopeks) when we get to Slippery," stipulated Itkin, who dearly loved a bargain and knew the boys would despise him for giving as much as they asked.

Squinty smiled cunningly.

"Eight griven (80 kopeks)," he said.

"Five griven when we get to Slippery," maintained Itkin steadily, and made as if to turn on his heel.

"Go on, Squinty," cried several voices. "Don't be a fool."

"All right," said Squinty suddenly.

"Will you come with me in a sledge?" asked Itkin.

"No fear," was the prompt reply, greeted with a volley of laughter, and cries of: "Squinty's not such a fool as he looks!" "Good old Squinty!"

"But it's too far to walk," objected Itkin.

"You take a sledge and I'll get there before you," said the boy. And Itkin had to content himself with this assurance.

When the sledge which he had taken arrived at the Stone Bridge it was assaulted by two little flying figures. Itkin kept his nose well into his collar, and his hat over his brows.

"Uncle dear," same the well-known snuffling whine, "Give us a kopek for a bit of bread. We haven't had a bit of bread the whole day! Noble Uncle, you are so rich, you wouldn't never miss a kopek for a poor hungry boy! Son of a bitch! Dirty Jew! Yah! Who got the skivvy a kid at Christmas? Can't spare a kopek for a poor boy! Rot in your fat then, lousy old swine!"

It was Slippery and Squinty working the bridge in harmony.

Once over the bridge Itkin dismissed the sledge and returned a few yards on foot.

"Come on, you two little devils," he called cheerfully.

"Now are you going to tell me what you know?" he asked.

The three were soon ensconced in the same eating-house in which Slippery had written out credentials for Itkin the night before. "How is it you're so certain Dolidzey didn't murder Pavlov?"

"Because he was alive after she was seen in the street," said Slippery.

"How do you know that?"

"*She* was seen in the Red Square at a quarter past one, and at half past one *he* was still alive."

"But how do you know that? Did you see him?"

"We heard him," said Slippery briefly.

Itkin leant forward eagerly.

"You tell him, Squinty," said Slippery.

"It was like this," said Squinty. "Me and Slippery and Black-Mug (Peter you know) has for a long time been in the habit of getting on to Pavlov's balcony, just under his window, and hearing him play his gramophone, which he did very well, didn't he, Slippery?"

"Very well, indeed," confirmed Slippery.

"Well, so Saturday night, as usual, we went there about one o'clock, which was his usual time for playing to us, and he hadn't begun. But we waited for him, not being in a hurry to catch a train, or anything of that sort, and he began just after the quarter struck, you can hear it plain from the Spassky Tower."

Itkin gazed from one to another of the pinched and eager faces before him. Was this indeed proof that Dolidzey had not murdered Pavlov? He knew that the man had been murdered sitting at the gramophone—if the boys had really heard him play after Dolidzey had left, then here was proof positive. Moreover, no one could have touched the gramophone after the murder, since the body had been found with the head resting on the sound-box. So if anyone had been heard to use the gramophone after Dolidzey's departure it must, humanly speaking, have been Pavlov himself, and he must have been stabbed by another hand, albeit with Tamara's dagger.

But how were the boys to prove that they had heard Pavlov play the gramophone, and that they had heard him after Dolidzey had left? They might have been mistaken in the time—or lying. Itkin did not believe the latter, for all motive was missing, but how convince others that they were not giving evidence for a bribe?

"Perhaps he was playing for Tamara?" he suggested.

"She was seen in the Red Square at a quarter past one," said Slippery.

"Oh, you might have been mistaken in the time," said Itkin carelessly.

"The watchman knows we ran into the yard *after* he saw Dolidzey come out," said Squinty sapiently.

"Squinty, my lad, you have a lawyer's mind," said Itkin enthusiastically.

He was getting on. There was plain evidence that Dolidzey had been seen to leave Pavlov's rooms *before* the boys ran into the yard. The boys said they had heard Pavlov play the gramophone after this. Pavlov had undoubtedly used his gramophone that night: he had been murdered in the act of putting on a new record. If only the boys' evidence could be corroborated, what an alibi for Dolidzey! He had a sudden inspiration.

"What was he playing? Could you make out?" he said eagerly.

Might not the whole alibi stand or fall by the identification of the song *on the other side of the record*? For this was a secret possibly known to none but this unsuspected audience and the Procurator himself.

"Ei ookhnem," said the boys unhesitatingly.

The song of the bent and sorefooted bargemen of the Volga, lifting their voices in pathetic resignation, all unconscious that one day their primitive refrain would echo wherever a gramophone can penetrate!

"If we can prove all this," said Itkin in the greatest excitement, "then we shall get Dolidzey off. Are you fellows prepared to swear to what you have just told me?"

The boys looked at each other doubtfully.

"Who's going to believe street-boys," said Slippery sadly. "They'll say we killed him ourselves. It wouldn't do for us to get before a beak. We shouldn't never get away again. They don't let you go once they've got you, the beaks don't."

"But if I give you my word of honour that you will not suffer for it?"

Slippery shook his head.

"No good, Uncle Julius," he said. "*We* trust you. But they wouldn't believe you. They'd find something to get us locked up for. If it wasn't murder it'd be stealing. That's certain."

For half an hour Itkin argued, threatened and promised. But all in vain. The boys wouldn't hear of putting their noses inside a police court, or giving evidence before a District Procurator.

"You tell them about it yourself," suggested Squinty encouragingly, moved by the little man's despair.

"Ah, that's not enough!" cried Itkin. "Look here, boys, are you going to let a girl—a poor working girl—suffer for what she never did—what you *know* she never did—when you could save her with a word? Do you realise that you are the only people in the world who *could* save her?"

The boys thought deeply, but again shook their heads and sighed. They could not and would not enter police premises, especially now Black-Mug had been nabbed. They were not sure that they themselves were not "wanted" in connection with Peter's little affair.

"Look here!" said Itkin, visited with a sudden idea. "If Vladimir Antonovich himself gives his word that no harm shall come to you, and that you'll be asked no questions except about your evidence in the Pavlov murder, will you give evidence before the District Procurator?"

Vladimir Antonovich was the Director of the Labour Colony. He was known far and wide by all the street boys in Moscow, and they trusted him implicitly *out* of prison, since, like Itkin, he had never once exploited his private friendships or personal knowledge to get any of them nabbed, although, like Itkin, he had more than once had the opportunity. The boys looked at one another. Then, to Itkin's immense relief, Squinty gave a solemn nod of assent.

Chapter XIII

HIS MASTER'S VOICE

ITKIN TOOK THE first opportunity after this momentous conversation to visit the Procurator and acquaint him with the result of his research. That gentleman naturally heard him with the greatest interest, but with a certain scepticism that, although the newspaper man understood to be natural, nevertheless exasperated him. He was privately convinced of the truth and finality of the evidence.

"I should like to see them, and hear their story myself," said the Procurator. "Indeed it is of course essential that I see them with the least possible delay. No one would be happier than I to find Tam—Dolidzey—provided with a satisfactory alibi. By the way, what do you think of the possibility of the young limbs having done it themselves?"

Itkin shook his head.

"No, their ringleader—Black-Mug Peter—was caught rifling a food store a week later," he said. "And he was caught because he was in a state of collapse from malnutrition and almost unable to run fifty yards. That doesn't lok like murder for robbery. The whole lot are down and out just now—not an extra crust among them. If these boys get money the first thing they do is to spend it on food and drink. And nobody's been drunk for a fortnight. You can always tell—their drinking bouts always end in an arrest or two. And it is quite impossible that they should not have had a bout after a haul like a stolen pocket-book."

"I bow to your superior and exhaustive knowledge of the subject," smiled the Procurator.

"Another thing," said Itkin eagerly. "Pavlov was stabbed in the jugular with scientific neatness. You could hardly expect any of my boys to make such a neat job of it. They're ready enough with their 'finnkas' I admit, but I doubt if they know so exactly the most vulnerable place in the human body."

"Bring your young men along to-morrow, by all means. Perhaps we shall be able to establish something."

"One moment," said Itkin: "I wonder if you'll be kind enough to satisfy my curiosity. Do just take out the record which poor Pavlov was playing when murdered. If the other side turns out to be 'The Volga Boat Song', won't you find it, to say the least of it, a somewhat striking coincidence?"

"Ha! There's something in that," said the Procurator.

He unlocked the cupboard in which he was at present keeping the Pavlov archives. and drew out a brown volume of gramophone records. A black disc in the usual envelope, worn off at one corner, as if from constant use, was tied by a piece of string to the outside of the album.

"The record he was just preparing to play when murdered was a song out of 'The Prophet', sung by Chaliapin. None of us who heard it go off by itself when we lifted the poor devil's head are likely to forget that," said the Procurator, drawing in his breath at the memory of that ghostly incident, as he undid the string. "Yes, here it is. 'The Prophet: Sung by Fedor Chaliapin'." He turned the record over. "What have we here? By Jove! Your little friends are right, Itkin! 'The Volga Boat Song', sung by Fedor Chaliapin!'"

"Aha! Aha!" exclaimed the newspaper man, fairly dancing in front of the desk in his excitement. "We're getting on, friend Procurator, we're getting on."

"Not so fast," said Nikulin with a smile. "There are other ways in which you, or anyone might have found out what was on the back of that record, you know."

"Oh, yes, of course, there are," said Itkin. "You might have told me yourself, but you didn't, you know. Or somebody else who was in the room with you might have told me that the gramophone went on playing the song from 'The Prophet' and I might have had the same record at home and turned it over to see what was on it, but I haven't and so I didn't. Or I might have a friend who knew a man who has English gramophone records, and *he* might have told me what was on the other side of the 'Prophet' record, but I haven't and I didn't."

The Procurator smiled again.

"I may say, Julius Cæsarovich, that I am prepared to take any statement made by you as bona fide," he said, "but it wouldn't do for me to be too credulous in my profession, you know."

The little man's face cleared.

"I am very grateful to you, Comrade Procurator," he said flushing. "I hope I shall always enjoy your good opinion."

More journeys by tram for Mr. Itkin, another visit to the Labour Colony, another search for Squinty and Slippery, but at last everything was in train for the fateful interview. In the meantime, the Procurator, despite his professed (and indeed actual) confidence in the newspaper man, had questioned the doctor and found that he had forgotten the song played on the gramophone, remembering only that the singer had been Chaliapin. The Morgue men remembered only the doctor's exclamation. Moreover, the Procurator had the doctor's word that he had mentioned the incident to no one and had never met Itkin.

The boys stood scared and silent, looking round them suspiciously. The three men—Vladimir Antonovich had willingly agreed to be present—looked alert and interested.

"Now I'm not going to ask you boys anything just yet," said the Procurator. "I'm going to give you a little treat and play you some tunes that you'll like, I'm sure."

The pinched faces reflected mingled doubt and delight. The Procurator put on one record after another, choosing as much as possible folk music, and watched the happy recognition and bewilderment chase each other like sun and shadow over the boys' countenances. They listened intently, and Itkin noticed how Squinty was involuntarily beating time with one grubby hand against his side. Then the Procurator put on a record that brought an expression of increased attention on the faces he was studying so intently. Their look of vague beatific enjoyment was sharpened into alertness. It was *The Volga Boat Song*. After a few bars, however, a disappointed, relaxed expression stole over Squinty's face, while Slippery continued to listen with knit brows. As soon as the song was over the Procurator quietly turned over the record, winding up the gramophone as if for another. But Squinty suddenly interrupted him.

"That's what he was playing on Saturday night," he said, but somewhat diffidently as if needing confirmation. "Wasn't it, Slippery?"

"Ye-es," said Slippery.

To his horror Itkin saw that the boys did not seem certain. He fidgeted uneasily in his chair. Not for such uncertain testimony had he hoped.

"Are you quite sure?" said the Procurator, turning to Slippery. The boys exchanged glances.

"That was what he *sang*," said Squinty slowly, "But you didn't play it as nice as what *he* did."

The Procurator smiled. He removed the record without a word, and replaced it by another from an envelope at his elbow. He set the disc in motion. The same song, the same words rang through the small office, but there was another quality in the voice, the careless, passionate bass, with its full, free rhythm. All felt the striking difference.

"That's right," cried the boys simultaneously, "that's him! That's what he played."

The three men laughed outright. Here was proof enough—no acting in the world could have reproduced that genuine recognition, that lighting of the dull faces.

"Well, they know the master's voice all right," said the Procurator.

"Wait, you fellows, I want a word with you," cried Vladimir Antonovich, starting up and following the boys who, their services suitably rewarded, were making off, as if they thought the sooner they left such an unhealthy neighbourhood the better for all concerned.

"He wants to persuade them to come and be made good citizens of," said Itkin ironically. "He'll never do it. They'll stay in the streets till they drop from starvation or get nabbed breaking the law."

He was elated at the success of his efforts and felt a not unnatural curiosity to know what the immediate effect would be for the imprisoned girl.

"Are you going to let her out?" he asked the Procurator when they found themselves alone.

"I shall release her from arrest certainly," said the Procurator, slowly, as if he were thinking out his plans while he spoke. "Her alibi satisfies me, and we have been unable to trace any money to her beyond the 100 rubles which she handed over at once and for which she gave at any rate a feasible account. Moreover, her character and her past are good and—I confess it—her statement made a great impression on me at the time. There is much in her favour, much. But I shall have to keep her under observation for a while. Things are looking black against Dubinsky just now, and it is by no means out of the question that they have been accomplices."

He touched a bell as he spoke, and gave instructions for Dolidzey to be sent to him. The official answering the bell returned in a few minutes with a report from the prison doctor to the effect that Dolidzey had been in a state of semi-collapse for the last two days and was unfit for cross-examination.

"Who told him I want to cross-examine her?" said Nikulin irritably. "Ask Dr. Popov to come and speak to me."

When the doctor appeared it was with a grave face.

"The organism is sorely tried," he reported. "Sorely. For the first week she seemed, as you know, stunned and obstinate. She seemed to have experienced great relief by the writing of that statement which was sent to you, but since she has heard nothing —she evidently placed great hopes in your being convinced of her innocence on reading the document—she has fallen into a heavy, coma-like depression, and can hardly be induced to take her food."

"But I have something I should like to consult you about, doctor," said the Procurator earnestly. "Citizen Itkin here has placed evidence in my hands to-day which amounts practically to an alibi for Dolidzey, and I have decided to release her, only keeping her under observation. Do you think her fit for immediate release?"

The doctor still looked grave.

"It might be a risk for her to return to the hard life which must be hers, I imagine, with no one to look after her. I would advise at least a week in a sanatorium, during which she can gradually realise her good fortune."

"You think the effects of the shock so serious?" said the Procurator. "She struck me as such a strong girl."

The doctor shook his head, still with his unconquerable gravity.

"Superficial impression," he said. "The frame looks sturdy enough, I grant you. Comes of good stock, perhaps. But there is no power of resistance, no stamina. Sapped by years of constant under-nourishment. Breaks at the first strain. Great mistake to think that peasants and primitive peoples are stronger than the cultivated classes. No margin of energy, no reserve of strength."

"Well, do you think I could break the good news to her to-night? Let her at least go to bed happy."

So Dolidzey was sent for. Itkin, who had never seen her before, thought she looked ill and depressed, but the Procurator was fairly shocked at the disastrous change in her appearance. The dusky skin had gone grey, the black eyes looked out from dark blue rings, the lips were puckered and wrung and her cheeks actually hollowed.

"Sit down, Tamara," he said kindly. "And don't look at me as if you thought I wanted to bite you. You should have told us the whole truth from the very beginning, you know, and it might have been better for yourself."

"I wrote you the whole truth," said the girl in a half-whisper.

"Perhaps you did, but you told a foolish story at first which no one could believe and which could therefore only do you harm in our eyes. However, I have good news for you. Pavlov has been proved to have been alive after you were seen to leave his house, and therefore the charge of murder is unconditionally withdrawn and you are free."

"Free!" she cried, and the tone of incredulous joy in her voice almost brought tears into the eyes of the men. "Do you mean I can go home—now?"

No question of gradually realising her happiness, thought Itkin.

"You can go as soon as Dr. Popov thinks you fit."

She looked wildly from face to face.

"*Fit!*" Her scorn was superb. "Does he think I shall be better here than at home?"

She cast a withering glance at the slight figure of the doctor, a glance that made Itkin think that she still had a little stamina left in her.

"D'you mean I can go home—right now?" she asked.

The Procurator wrote a few words on a slip of paper.

"Take this with you and show it to the Chief Wardress," he said, "but come back here again for a minute before you leave. You must leave me your signature here, you know."

The girl was out of the room with the piece of paper, almost before the smiling guard who had accompanied her could follow her. She was back again with a small bundle under her arm in less than ten minutes. The men all gazed at her. Gone was the shrinking beaten creature of ten minutes ago, her place taken by a girl with flashing eyes and blazing cheeks. Even the flaccid hair seemed to have sprung into wild life and stood around her face like a dark halo.

"What day is it to-day, Citizen Procurator?" she asked, her voice firm and ringing. "I've lost count of everything sitting here."

The Procurator consulted the calendar on his desk and told her it was Thursday.

"Ha!" She shook her head like a horse sniffing the battle. "Then to-morrow there'll be a rehearsal at nine for *The Lake of Swans* and I shall be just in time."

She signed her name where the Procurator indicated, with trembling fingers, shook hands in her excitement with all the men in turn, murmuring, she knew not why: "Thank you! Thank you!" and was gone with a rush of her short skirts and a violent bang of the door.

"Well, doctor," said the Procurator. "Stamina seems all right, eh?"

"Fortunately, nature is always putting us doctors in the wrong," said the doctor philosophically. "Only yesterday, our family cat ran a needle into its tongue, God knows how. Nobody knew what was the matter with the poor beast till I got home and then I had to take it out in three pieces. I told my daughter not to worry if the animal was unable to eat for a day or two, but to put down a saucer of warm milk and give it no solid food. And I'm blessed if that darned cat didn't jump on to the table while I was speaking and eat up the chop that was waiting for my supper."

They were all glad to laugh, but the Procurator, secretly sentimental, remembered a pot of cyclamen which he had put outside his door two days ago to be thrown away as dead, its white petals soft and flabby, its beauty extinguished, and how the charwoman, instead of throwing it away, had stood it in a bowl of water, and in an hour it was blooming again, every petal taut like a little sail.

CHAPTER XIV

"SAY I'M GROWING OLD, BUT ADD— 'JENNY KISSED ME'"

A NATURAL CURIOSITY, as well as a love of the ballet natural to all good citizens of the ancient town of Moscow, drew Mr. Itkin to the Grand Theatre on Sunday, when *The Lake of Swans* was advertised. As well as curiosity and devotion to the ballet, however, he had another and stronger motive. Impelled by natural sympathy and the gratitude he felt for Itkin's services, the Procurator had let him into the details of the case, and the little man's chivalrous nature was now fired with the desire to extricate Dubinsky, who, some instinct told him, was no more responsible for the murder of Pavlov than Tamara. That they had been accomplices he did not for a moment believe and he thought he saw that the Procurator did not seriously entertain the idea himself.

The theatre was full and the dance of the six swans, a brisk affair of tip-toes and prancing heels, not particularly suggestive of swans or any other fowl, but none the less delightful and full of verve, was led by Tamara herself. This dance is always a favourite with the public and they acclaimed it generously. Itkin felt an absurd personal pride when, after the applause had died down he heard his neighbour say: "The little dark one is great," to a friend who answered carelessly: "Why, yes, that's Dolidzey. They think no end of her in the theatre."

There were few public buildings in Moscow in which Mr. Itkin didn't know his way about, and probably not a single theatre. With the ease born of long practice he caught a lingering youth and dispatched him with his card, on which he scribbled under his name, "Interested in Dubinsky", to Tamara. In a few minutes she was before him, in all the horrors of stage make-up at close quarters, but with her dark eyes alive in the mask of powder and grease. She smiled frankly at Itkin and put out her hand.

"You were there when the Procurator let me go and you wished me good luck. I didn't thank you then. I do now."

"Well, I don't think you need much wishing," he remarked with simple admiration. "The whole theatre was talking of you as the rising star of the ballet."

She blushed, with devastating results to her make-up.

"You want to tell me something about Dubinsky?" she said hastily, as if embarrassed by his simple compliment.

"I wanted to *ask* you about him. I thought perhaps you could put me in the way of establishing his innocence, as I did yours."

Her eyes were round with astonishment.

"You?"

"Why, yes. So that's why I feel a sort of right to your co-operation."

"Oh, for that matter I'd do anything I could in any case," she said, speaking quickly and nervously. "That is, of course. But now I've got to go, that bell was for me. Will you be at the stage-door after the show to-night?"

Mr. Itkin had a taxi ready at the stage-door and they drove to the Writers' Club, which is housed in a small mansion with a verandah, a long garden protecting it from the noise and dust of the street. It was easy enough to find a secluded corner in the almost deserted dining room, where they could talk undisturbed. Tamara delighted her host by asking for a steak and a glass of beer, and showing herself well able to deal with both, as well as a plate of black bread.

"It won't prevent you sleeping?" he asked a little anxiously, watching enormous mouthfuls rapidly disappearing. Fork in air, knife slanting upwards from the rim of the table in her clenched fist, she displayed her white teeth in a frank smile.

"I feel as if nothing would prevent me sleeping again. Just as in prison I felt as if I should never be able to sleep the night through again."

"Well, about Dubinsky," he began. "Perhaps you'll tell me all you know, or perhaps you'll just let me tell you, very shortly, how I was able to get your innocence established, so that you feel confidence in me, and realise that I want to do the same for your comrade."

"But I'm just dying to hear," she assured him.

She listened with her glowing eyes fixed on his face, and when he described to her the cross-country journeys with reference letters from street boys (she insisted on every step of the proceedings being described to her in detail) she jumped up and seating herself on the empty chair beside Itkin, threw her arms round his neck, and bestowed upon him a hearty kiss. No one saw except a waiter just entering the room and he only looked delighted.

"You good man," said Tamara fervently, gazing with moist eyes at her saviour.

"Now, now, my dear girl," he said, touched and embarrassed. "It's those boys you've got to thank, not me."

"Yes, indeed," she repeated. "How can I ever thank them? I must join the Committee for the Liquidation of Vagrancy. I will to-morrow."

"They'd much rather be danced to than liquidated," he said comically. "We'll organise something together, won't we? Get them to the theatre, or something."

The way was now cleared for the discussion of Dubinsky's fate. To Itkin's astonishment Tamara told him that she had only heard the day before of his arrest. On Friday, at the rehearsal, everybody had been so glad to see her, and so full of the miracle of her release, that they had been afraid to spoil her first joy by mentioning the unfortunate Dubinsky, of whose arrest, moreover, they thought she must have heard herself in prison.

"And didn't you wonder where he was?" asked Itkin in surprise. "I thought he was your particular admirer."

"Well, I'm ashamed to say I was so drunk with joy that I forgot his very existence," she confessed. "And all yesterday I was so busy rehearsing I simply couldn't find out anything about him. I tried to see the Procurator to-day, but he'd gone into the country for the day, and will only be back to-morrow after midday."

Itkin was pleased to find that she had not left her old companion to his fate.

"Well, now, let's have your theory," he said.

"About what? If you mean, who killed Pavlov? I haven't the ghost of a notion. If you mean, was it Dubinsky? Well, of course, I'm perfectly sure, as every sane person must be, that he had absolutely nothing to do with it. Can you tell me what on earth made them arrest him?"

"Well, in the first place," said Itkin, looking at her steadily, "he was outside Little Paul Street between twelve and two—or is at any rate unable to prove an alibi—just when the murder is supposed to have taken place."

"*Dubinsky* was?" she cried incredulously. "What on earth was he doing there?"

"*He* says he was watching for you to come out, and followed you home, and then went back again to his lodgings, which are, as you probably know, not very far from Little Paul Street. Anyhow, he is known to have got home about two, and was out during the fatal hours."

"But how is it I never saw him?"

"He stayed on the other side of the road. He says you forbade him to follow you."

"Yes. I told him I would never speak to him again," mused the girl. "Well, Dubinsky, of all the silly asses! Why on earth didn't he do as he was told and go quietly to bed? I *told* him that it would be the worse for him if he did, and it has been. But, still, I don't quite understand what they think. That he saw me come out and nipped up to do Pavlov in with my dagger, which he found nice and handy?"

"That's more or less the idea."

"But—why should he exactly?"

"Ah! That's just it! Just as in your case, there is an apparent, or perhaps I should say a possible motive. *You* might have been supposed to kill Pavlov out of revenge for his assault and stolen the money as an afterthought, while Dubinsky, poor chap, is now under suspicion of having killed him from motives of jealousy, and stolen the money to make it look like a burglary."

"I see-ee. And is that all they have against him—that he was in the street at that time? They might as well say the same of the night watchman."

"Well, of course, the night watchman did fall under suspicion just at first—"

"But he wasn't arrested!" interrupted the girl quickly.

"No, he wasn't arrested," agreed Itkin quietly. "But then there wouldn't have been sufficient motive and *he* has since disposed of no sum of money."

"And Dubinsky has?" she flashed out.

"And Dubinsky has."

"Ah!" she cried. "How much?"

"On the day after the murder—the Monday—he paid his landlady the rent and a few rubles over, after having owed her for three months or more."

"But his uncle from Kiev might have sent him the money!" cried the girl, her brows knit in distress.

"His uncle from Kiev sent him 100 rubles on the Tuesday nearly three weeks *after* he had paid his rent," said Itkin inexorably.

"Wait a minute! Hold on a minute!" exclaimed Tamara, clutching at her black head. "You said he paid her on Monday, two days after the murder. Let me see—Saturday morning, Sunday before the show, Monday—" she drummed her fingers on the table, evidently working at calculations. "Yes, that comes out all right. I can explain to you how he had the money to pay on Monday, Julius Cæsarovich, for I gave it to him myself on Sunday evening, just before the show—on the day on which I was arrested."

Itkin could hardly believe his ears.

"You gave it him?" he gasped. "You?"

She nodded.

"M'hm. I did. I put it into his hands myself. Two hundred rubles."

"And are you ready to tell the Procurator so yourself?"

"Of course I must tell him if that's what Dubinsky got nabbed for."

"And can you account for the money satisfactorily? Can you tell him where you got it from yourself?"

"I can tell him I did *not* get it from Pavlov," she returned equably.

"Can you *prove* it, girl?" whispered Itkin, looking round nervously. He was relieved to see that there was no one within ear-shot.

"I—I *could*, easily enough," she answered with some hesitation. "But I'd rather not—at least Dubinsky wouldn't like it if I did."

"But, my God, child, do you realise that you've told me enough to get yourself rearrested, as accomplice this time. And mind you that's just exactly what they're on the look out for."

A hunted look passed over her face for a moment. Then she shook back her massive black hair and laughed shortly.

"But you won't, I know," she said calmly.

"I won't what?"

"Tell on me," she said, lowering her voice.

The sweat broke out on Itkin's forehead. He plunged for his handkerchief and dabbed feverishly at his brow.

"What a child you are," he said. "Can't you see my position? You confide in me awful things like this and make me almost an accessory after the fact—"

"Now don't get yourself all worked up," she said soothingly. "It isn't so bad as all that. I mean I really can prove to you where I got the money from, but Dubinsky wouldn't *like* it if I did. It might be almost as bad for him."

"Won't you let me judge for myself?" pleaded Itkin.

"Well, will you promise not to split?"

He reflected, then gave the promise, considering her to be sufficiently Dubinsky's friend to allow herself to be persuaded if necessary to produce any evidence that might be in his favour.

"All right, then," continued Tamara in a lowered voice. "I'll trust you. Well, then, on Saturday, I got 400 marks through the post from Germany and went to the Bank and changed them into rubles, and on Sunday, just before the show, I put them into Dubinsky's hand, for they were from his cousin in Berlin, who sent them to me for him."

"Why didn't he send them straight to Dubinsky if they were meant for him?" interrupted Itkin.

"I'll tell you if you give me half a chance," said Tamara. "This cousin, you see, works on a counter-revolutionary paper in Berlin, and Dubinsky didn't like getting money from him regularly, so whenever the cousin had any money to send, Dubinsky used to give him a different address to send it to. This time he gave him *my* address. He asked me first, and I let him, of course, but I don't believe you'll ever find out who got the money for him the other times, for no one will want to admit it, and Dubinsky would never give them away."

"And do you remember the exact date when you got this money?"

"Of course. I told you—Saturday morning—the day of the murder itself."

"So the post-office receipt could be traced," said Itkin thoughtfully.

"I suppose so. But I don't know what Dubinsky would say to my giving him away."

"But is it such a crime to receive money from abroad?"

"Well, no, not in itself, of course. But it's rather a special case. You see, only about a year ago, they found out somehow that this Dubinsky in Berlin was our Dubinsky's cousin, and then he swore himself black and blue that he never had any communication with him, and they gave him a sort of warning. And he really doesn't, but he simply can't bear to refuse a little money now and then, for the poor boy is absolutely stony and his cousin really owes him the money, for he took all Dubinsky's mother's jewels abroad with him."

"But, good heavens!" cried Itkin with feeling, "wouldn't a man rather be accused of having money from anyone—even a counter-revolutionary relation—to which he had the right, than of having murdered a man in cold blood and robbed him?"

"You'd think so, wouldn't you?" agreed the girl. "But you see he didn't say anything himself to clear him of the suspicion of murder. I wonder—"

She seemed to check herself.

"What?" asked Itkin, struck by a change in her expression.

"Do you think the young ass purposely said nothing, so as to distract suspicion from me?" she said thoughtfully. "Now I wonder if it was that."

"Well, now, that's at least a theory," said Itkin warmly. "And I wouldn't be surprised if it wasn't feasible."

"At first," proceeded Tamara meditatively, "he would in any case try to hide the fact of having the money from his cousin. He'd hope it needn't come out."

"Quite right," said Itkin. "He said he got it from his uncle, and when this was discovered to be untrue he didn't like to admit his perjury immediately—"

"No," interrupted Tamara excitedly, "and then when he thought it over, he thought he could always produce the evidence of the money at any time, and in the meantime, perhaps they would let me go."

"Why, yes!" cried Itkin. "Now I come to think of it, I remember Nikulin told me that the first thing Dubinsky asked him was, what was the good of their keeping you both."

"That's it!" said Tamara, clapping the palms of her hands

together. "Partly he doesn't want to give himself away about the money, partly he wants to shield *me*. Well, now, what are we going to do about it?"

"For my part," said Itkin gravely, "I can see nothing better than laying the whole story before the Procurator."

Tamara frowned thoughtfully.

"And then what?"

"And then let him decide. It's no good, Tamara Geyorgyevna," he said urgently, "you need have no illusions. What*ever* happens now, they'll keep the boy till they make him account for the possession of the money. He lied about it—ergo, he has something to conceal—ergo, the police have something to discover."

"I suppose you're right," said Tamara reluctantly.

They parted with mutual liking and a warm handshake. Tamara promised to try and see the Procurator the next day.

The Procurator seemed somewhat surprised to see her, but showed immediate interest when she hinted at information regarding Dubinsky's money. He asked several searching questions and she was quick enough to see that he was cross-examining her, and trying to see if she would contradict herself. At last he seemed satisfied as to the truthfulness of her answers.

"Now what are you going to do?" she asked him flatly.

"First of all I'm going to think all this over," he said, bending whimsical brows upon this girl whom he had known so abject and who now seemed so brisk and independent.

"I've thought it all over already," she announced calmly.

"And may I ask for your conclusions?"

She was not at all slow to favour him with these.

"First of all you'll cross-examine Dubinsky again," she said promptly. "In the light of the information I've just given you. And you'll be making a great mistake."

"Oh, I will, will I?"

"Of course you will! Don't you see he may still go on lying from the same motive that's making him lie now—to shield me."

"Oh, you think it's that, do you?" asked the Procurator, looking with interest at the confident young face.

"Well, don't you?" she countered.

"I confess it *had* crossed my mind," he admitted.

"Well, then, don't you see by *your* method you'll get no further?"

"But if I let him know that you are already released?"

"How is he to know that I will not be rearrested if he clears himself?" she rallied smartly.

"Young lady, you are wasted on the ballet," he murmured. "We want you here. Well, now what do you suggest?"

"I suggest that you let somebody in the prison casually tell Dubinsky that my alibi has been proved, and that I've been released, and see if he doesn't make a clean breast of the whole thing voluntarily—without being cross-examined again."

"Ha!" said the Procurator, "very neat. Very neat indeed. As soon as he hears you are released he is to take steps to clear himself. Is this a signal between you, pre-arranged?"

For a moment the girl, who coloured all over her face and neck, seemed struck dumb. Then she became deadly pale and broke out into passionate, almost incoherent speech.

"You don't mean that!" she cried. "What's the good of insulting me, when I only want to tell you all I know? You know I couldn't have murdered Pavlov, and you've nothing else against me."

Nikulin shot a steady glance at her, but said nothing. He pressed a bell-push on his desk.

"At the moment I am interested to prove that the money you mentioned was received from the post office on the date you give —the day before the murder. In the meantime I fear I must detain you for half an hour or so."

Tamara's wrath seemed to have subsided as suddenly as it had sprung up.

"Well, it isn't the first time you've done that," she said placidly.

The ubiquitous Yanovitsky, who appeared in response to the bell, was sent to make the necessary inquiries at the post office, which he did with his usual celerity and thoroughness. Tamara's story having been so far confirmed, she was once more set at liberty.

When, after the Procurator had carefully ascertained that Dubinsky was aware of Tamara's release, that young man made no voluntary statement, he felt disappointment. He had been secretly impressed by Tamara's arguments, and agreed with her in his heart that it would be better—more conclusive—if the confession were made voluntarily, and not as the result of cross-examination. When, however, the next day passed with no sign of life from Dubinsky, the Procurator had him sent for. Confinement and suspense had told upon the youth even more quickly than it had upon Tamara. He looked ghastly, and as if on the verge of a breakdown.

"I sent for you to see if you had anything fresh to tell me," said the Procurator.

"We don't get much news where I am," said the young man, with a touch of grim humour.

"But still you sometimes see old things in a new light, down there," said the Procurator equally grimly. "I thought perhaps you might feel like telling me where you got the 200 rubles from that you *didn't* get from Kiev."

Silence. Suddenly: "Is Dolidzey really released?"

"Aha!" thought Nikulin. "So Tamara was right. Smart girl!"

"I thought you knew that," he said quietly, not taking his eyes off the boy's face.

"I heard it was so, but I thought it might be a ruse to make me confess."

The Procurator pounced on him.

"So you have something to confess," he said.

Dubinsky smiled wearily.

"About this wretched money, you know."

The Procurator leaned forward and tapped upon the desk with his pencil.

"Dolidzey is released," he said, "And she has told me the truth about the money. I want confirmation of her statement from you. Are you prepared to give it?"

The young man flushed, paled and flushed again. For a moment or two he fidgeted with a penholder and a paper-cutter on the desk, his long lashes resting on his cheek. He seemed to be in a kind of trance. Then suddenly he opened his grey eyes wide and looked straight at the Procurator and said something so naïve that that gentleman nearly laughed aloud:

"How am I to know what she told you?"

And yet not so naïve for he followed it up immediately with another question:

"How am I to know if she really told you anything at all?"

"Thinks I'm calling his bluff," was the Procurator's mental comment. "Not such a fool, this boy."

He opened a drawer in the desk.

"I have Dolidzey's signed statement here," he said. "Will that satisfy you?"

"But you won't show it to me first," said Dubinsky quickly. "You'll get a signed statement from me, and then you'll compare them."

Again a short bark of laughter from the Procurator. He seemed to think for a moment.

"I tell you what we'll do," he said. "I'll get Dolidzey here and you can satisfy yourself from her lips that she has told me the actual truth."

With this the interview ended, to be resumed the next day in the presence of Tamara.

"I told you it would be the worse for you if you followed me!" burst out that irrepressible young person as soon as she was brought face to face with her admirer. "You can't say I didn't give you fair warning."

The lad seemed too downcast to answer back and Nikulin hastened to give an official tone to the interview.

"Citizen Dolidzey," he said, as solemnly as possible, "are you prepared to swear that the signed statement you left with me yesterday is a true and exact account of the way in which Citizen Dubinsky became possessed of 200 rubles on the morning after the murder of Pavlov?"

"Yes," said Tamara steadily, looking at Dubinsky, who returned her gaze with distended eyeballs. "I am."

"Will you inform Citizen Dubinsky, without alluding to its contents, that you have made such a statement?"

"I told the Procurator how I came to give you the money, Dubinsky," said Tamara, turning towards the astonished lad, "because I and another person who believes in us both, and wishes you well, thought it was the only thing to do. Tell the Procurator the whole truth yourself, and then he'll see that it must have been so, if we both say so independently. Don't you see there's no other way, Dubinsky?"

For a moment Dubinsky was silent. Then he raised his head and looked straight at Tamara.

"All right," he said in a low voice, "Since you've told I might as well, I suppose."

He turned towards the Procurator, and began his tale in a toneless voice.

"About a fortnight before the day of the murder I wrote to my —a relation of mine living in Berlin, asking him to send me some money, as I had had nothing from my uncle for three months, and was in debt to my landlady and needed a pair of goloshes. My—relation—owed me a large sum of money and had only paid off a half of it. He sent me the money after some delay, and that is how I happened to pay my landlady on the day after the murder. And that's all—"

His voice trailed off and he glanced guiltily at Tamara.

The Procurator's voice cut across the tense silence.

"How did you receive this money?"

"Through the post."

"To what address was it sent?"

The Procurator intercepted a quick glance between the young people.

"To—a—a friend's."

"Why not to your own?"

"I preferred not to receive money from abroad."

"Can you give me this friend's name and address?"

"I can't."

"Why not?"

"I don't know if the friend whose address I used would like it to be known."

"Oh, spit it out!" exclaimed Tamara impatiently. "Can't you see he knows, anyhow? Why, I told him myself!"

The Procurator raised his hand with a warning look at the girl.

"But I'm only urging him to tell you everything, Procurator," she said.

"Well, then—it was Dolidzey herself who took the money for me," muttered the boy.

"And how did she transmit it to you?"

"She gave it to me just before the show on Sunday, the day she was arrested."

"And why did you not tell me all this at once?"

"I was confused. I didn't expect the whole affair about the money to come up."

"But afterwards, when it was found out that your uncle's money came afterwards, why did you not own up then?"

"Well, I thought I could clear myself any time and in the meantime, I thought perhaps Tama—Dolidzey—might somehow get away—as she did," he finished defiantly.

Tamara shot a triumphant glance at Nikulin. Was she not confirmed in every detail? "Now, are you going to let that silly ass go?" she murmured, her great black eyes at once mocking and imploring. And she did not leave until she had wrung out of the Procurator the admission that there was no longer sufficient ground for keeping Dubinsky under arrest, although they would both of them continue to be under observation and might expect to be called up for cross-examination should subsequent events demand this.

CHAPTER XV

"S" FOR SOKOLIN?

HAVING PRACTICALLY RULED out the girl Dolidzey and the boy Dubinsky as possible murderers of Arkady Petrovich Pavlov, the Procurator had to look out for substitutes. The idea of the mysterious "S" who had left the note on the dead man's desk and his possible connection with the "White Eagle" Society never left him. The question was where to begin to look for him. On the whole, the Procurator thought another visit to Miss Burova was indicated, both by the state of his nails and the dearth of evidence. Who knows, perhaps that apparently blameless and shallow-pated lady could a tale unfold if properly approached. Perhaps he had been hasty in dismissing her altogether from his mind? At the least, perhaps others of her clients might turn out to have been acquainted with Pavlov. Nikulin blamed himself for having neglected this channel, and allowing himself to be led astray by the cloud of circumstantial evidence against the young people from the Grand Theatre.

He chose five o'clock as a likely sort of time for a man to go to his manicurist after work, and once more selected his best tie and put scent on his handkerchief. Once again he stood before the door, looked up and down the shabby staircase, noted the reception hours of Dr. Sokolin, surgeon-dentist, and rang three times as bidden by a card under the bell, in order to summon Miss Burova, manicurist. This time the door was opened by a stout girl in a print frock and felt boots, who replied to his question that Miss Burova was at home. As he divested himself of his outer clothes, the familiar roar of the primus stove in the kitchen rushed to his ears and the smell pervading the tiny hall promised dinner to come for one or more of the several families inhabiting the flat. In the stuffy but cosy room that he remembered so vividly, a young lady was having the final touches put to her already glistening nails. The scent of pear-drops assailed the Procurator's nostrils, as the manicurist, with sacramental solemnity applied the final coating of celluloid with a tiny brush. Nikulin remembered that she had mentioned at his last visit that her clientèle was principally feminine. He noted the present specimen with interest: she was a sweet young thing, with brief hair and skirts that displayed her shining silk-stockinged knees as she sat, and when a man looked at her mouth he saw red. She tripped out of the room on high heels when released, and was heard engaging some unknown he in long and coquettish converse over the telephone in the passage.

"That's Luba Blok from the Little Theatre," said Miss Burova complacently. "Oh dear, you have let your nails go again."

This was just the opening Nikulin wanted.

"I expect you get a lot of theatrical people coming to you," he insinuated. "That must make your work very interesting."

"That's what I always say," she responded with animation. "I always say I wouldn't change my profession with anybody. I just sit here and all those interesting people that other people have to run after, come to me themselves without being asked."

A lavatory attendant might make a similar boast thought Nikulin, with an irrepressible twitch at the corner of his lips.

"But still, you know," continued Burova, with a pensive sigh, "it requires a lot of tact, my work."

"Really?" said Nikulin politely.

"Well, of course it does. Stands to reason," she said, steadily and mercilessly cutting away strips of skin from the base of his nail, causing him exquisite pain. "You see, with such a connection like I have, a girl can't be too careful, for of course theatrical people are very interesting and I'm sure they're often kindness itself, but they can be very funny, ve-ry funny. Your left hand, please."

She placed the fingers of his right hand in a bowl of soapy water, and rearranged a little cushion under his left elbow.

"Yes, they can be very funny indeed, you'd be surprised. Oh, dear, this hand of yours is a disgrace! I never did see a man let the skin grow up his nails like you do—never. Yes, as I was saying, they can be very funny, and I always try to make their appointments so's the wrong ones shouldn't by any chance meet each other. But accidents will happen sometimes, and then you never can tell how they'll behave. For instance, a friend of mine happened to come in to get her hands done the other day—I mean she's more in the florist line herself, and of course she must look after her hands, because when you're showing somebody flowers it might make a difference what sort of hands you have. I mean nicely-kept hands do set off a couple of roses or a sheaf of lilies of the valley, don't they? Well, so Volyina—you know, from the Bolshoï Theatre, Sophie Volyina—came in, just as it might be you, while I was still doing my friend's nails. And so my friend, being as I say more in the florist line herself, didn't recognise Volyina. I mean she does look quite another thing in real life, of course. And so this friend of mine said to Volyina: 'Excuse me, but it seems to me your stockings come from abroad. Perhaps you wouldn't be averse to sell me a pair or two at a reasonable price.' And of course Volyina drew herself up rather haughtily and said: 'I don't seem to understand you.' Only of course she really understood perfectly well, but what she meant was she didn't want any personal questions from my friend. So then my friend said: 'Oh, I'm sorry I spoke if it's a sore point. But if I didn't want my legs remarked upon I wouldn't wear such short skirts myself.' And of course Volyina has got very developed legs, I mean, ballet dancers always do. But what she couldn't understand was somebody not recognising her, but afterwards of course I explained that my friend was more in the florist line and then of course she understood. But it was awkward and just the kind of thing I always try to avoid."

"I see," said Nikulin, his head positively whirling in the attempt to follow the intricacies of the story. "And do you get actors as well as actresses?"

"Oh, yes, but not so much of course, because gentlemen are apt to be more impatient and they mostly would rather pay more to have their nails done at the hairdresser's, when they have their hair cut. But I do get some theatrical gentlemen. The head of the ballet department in the Bolshoï Theatre—his name is Gorbunov—he's one of what I call my regular customers."

"Is he, by Jove?" thought the Procurator.

"A good deal more regular than I am, I hope," he said aloud, with a polite laugh.

"Yes, well, I should hope he would be, if only for my sake," she said delivering up his left hand. "Because if most of my customers weren't a little bit more regular than you, it would be a pity about me, wouldn't it?"

There was humour, still more good humour, in the pale eyes. At that moment a knock at the door preceded the appearance of a burly gentleman in a surgeon's coat.

"Come in, Constantin Ivanovich," said the manicurist. 'I shall be free in one minute."

"Thank you, Elena Mihailovna," said the newcomer genially. "But I'm busy with patients till half-past seven to-day. I only looked in, between two of them, to know if nine o'clock would be too late for you to do my hands to-day."

"Oh dear, no," was the gracious response. "Nine o'clock isn't late for you and me, Constantin Ivanovich."

With a smile, and a vague bow in Nikulin's direction, the burly head was withdrawn and the door closed.

"Well, that wasn't an actor, I suppose," said the Procurator. "Have you change for a chervonetz, Elena Mihailovna?"

She had, and he noted that she took it all from the shallow little drawer in the manicurist's table, along with her scissors and files.

"So she makes as much as ten rubles some days; must be plenty of clients," he mentally registered.

"No, he's not an actor," she said, scrabbling with her long nails for the coins on the boards of the drawer. "He's a dentist. He has the next room to me, so you see it's very handy for him. I mean he can slip in whenever he has a spare moment, and of course he's very busy."

"Is he a good dentist? I need to have a tooth crowned and I keep putting it off because I really don't know anyone to go to."

If there is one passion common to human nature it is to get others to attend their own dentist. Miss Burova became positively enthusiastic in her praises of her neighbour's skill.

"Everybody who goes to him is satisfied," she said. "I'm sure the people I recommend to him are so thankful to me. Why I had a gentleman friend from America—oh, yes, well you used to know him, too, I mean poor Arkady Petrovich, you know, Pavlov —and he used to say that he couldn't get his teeth so well done in New York as he could by Sokolin."

"Quite right," said Nikulin energetically, "I remember he was always raving about some dentist and telling me I ought to go to him, but I never could remember his name."

"Well, you may be sure it was Sokolin," said Miss Burova

decidedly, "for he never went to any other dentist in Moscow. And they were very friendly, too, and Pavlov always said he was as good a fellow as he was a dentist and could judge a leg as well as he could a tooth."

"A leg?" repeated Nikulin mildly. "I'm afraid I don't quite catch—"

"Well, of course, he meant a leg in the ballet," said the lady. "Poor Arkady Petrovich was a great devotee to 'Terpsichore', as you know."

She looked exceedingly pleased with herself for having safely brought off the genteel allusion and bade her client goodbye in high good humour.

Outside the door he studied the plate in the centre that he had already noticed. "C. I. Sokolin, Dental-Surgeon. Artificial Teeth a Speciality. 10 to 3. 5 to 7.30 and by appointment." Vague but exciting speculations surged through the Procurator's mind. "S" a friend of Pavlov's. A fellow devotee of "Terpsichore". Had not "S" waited for Pavlov until he had to go to the theatre? Had he not, through the common kitchen, free access to Pavlov's house? He went home with his head in a whirl of combinations and permutations.

One thing emerged quite clearly: his teeth must be seen to. A few more murders, he reflected, and I shall be set up from head to foot. I wish—fingering his incipient tonsure—one of Pavlov's friends had been a hair specialist. However, I suppose I shall have to take them as I find them. Procurators can't be choosers and I have a left incisor that has long been crying out for a little skilled attention. Let us at least hope that Sokolin will live up to expectations as a dentist.

It was not difficult to make an appointment with Sokolin for the following day, and accordingly the Procurator found himself seated in the inquisitorial chair even sooner than was quite pleasant. Although the room bore unmistakable signs of having to serve as bedroom and living room, the corner devoted to dental surgery was well lighted and well appointed, and reassuringly clean. Sokolin himself inspired confidence, with his spotless coat, his plump well-kept hands and business-like expression.

Like all dentists he only became really conversational when he had his victim neatly gagged. Having plugged the Procurator with compact little sausages of cotton wool and fixed a wad of

hard rubber securely between his top and bottom jaws, he then
asked him, with insinuating grace, who had recommended him,
at the same time begging him, quite unnecessarily, on no account
to close his jaws. Nikulin could only roll his eyes wildly and raise
a hand in feeble gesture to intimate his impotence. The dentist
went on happily talking, picking up minute pills of paste in his
tweezers, discarding them with every appearance of fastidiousness
for others, suddenly dashing at his drill, causing the Procurator
acute discomfort for a few seconds, fiddling about again with the
pills and generally appearing, after the kind of dentists, to be
having a perfectly lovely time at the expense of his victim.
Following the burly figure with his eyes and catching sight every
now and then of a florid face with slightly protruding eyeballs,
the Procurator played idly with the idea of a sensational brochure
to be entitled: "The dentist: is he a criminal type?" in which
he would skilfully expound the theory that the dentist was a case
of successful sublimation of inherent sadistic impulses, and prove
with overwhelming statistics that, like the surgeon, the dentist,
frequently had the murderer's thumb. Sokolin's thumb just at
that moment was pressing mercilessly on Nikulin's jaw, while with
his forefinger he squeezed something soft and penetrating into
a hollow tooth, which made the Procurator thoroughly believe in
his theory—all except the sublimation part, that is—but next
moment, rinsing his weary mouth, spluttering and spitting into
the basin, he realised that it was a very different criminal he
was looking for—a possible murderer, it is true, but not
necessarily an inherent sadist, nor a criminal type. The whole
question seemed to him whether the letter "S" stood for Sokolin.

"You asked me who sent me to you," he said, as soon as he
could speak, choosing a time when he could keep a watchful eye
on the dentist's reflection in the glass. Sokolin was at the moment
energetically washing his plump white hands under the tap. The
Procurator was pretty sure it was not mere suggestion that made
him think that his remark was of special interest to the man.
How well he knew that look when the whole inner man suddenly
goes on guard, the brain sending a thousand subtle signals to
every muscle. The protruding eyes, which had been roving carelessly in their sockets, suddenly froze; the rhythmically revolving
hands remained clasped and still; the mouth, which had been
relaxed and easy, shut like a trap, the unconsciously tapping boot

was hushed. It even seemed to the watcher that the florid face had gone a shade paler, but he couldn't be quite sure of that. It was, however, perfectly obvious that the whole man had leapt to attention at a single signal. Undoubtedly a man with a secret to guard, and ready to fly to its defence at an instant's notice.

"It was your neighbour and—I think—our mutual manicurist," said the Procurator, smiling and watching with interest the obvious relief that spread over the whole man. As in the nursery legend of the old woman and the pig, when everything proceeded normally the very moment "the cow began to drink the water", all Sokolin's muscles resumed their interrupted play: the hands went on revolving under the tap, the lips relaxed into the slight smile that was apparently almost habitual to them, the eyeballs moved freely in their sockets, the tapping boot resumed some rhythm known only to it. Sokolin smiled again, and at that moment caught the Procurator's eye upon his reflection in the looking-glass. Did some expression of alarm creep into those protruding eyeballs, or was it merely the Procurator's suggestible state of mind that made him interpret the dentist's expression thus? However that might be it seemed to him that the man's eyes said: "Have you been watching me all the time?" Then he remembered that that is quite a natural state of mind for anyone caught unawares in a mirror. He hastened to let his own features be inundated with a sly smile as he said knowingly:

"A very expert lady, that. I thought a recommendation from her worth having."

The florid face relaxed into something like a broad grin, and then the Procurator was sure that he had really paled before, for a distinct added richness suffused the slightly flabby cheeks.

Having paid for his treatment, or ill treatment, as he thought ruefully (for he felt by no means sure that Sokolin's skill justified his friend's high praise), and made an appointment for the next day, the Procurator went out thoughtfully, the speculations with which his head was filled successfully distracting his attention from his aching jaw. At first he started off mechanically in the direction of his office, and then suddenly, struck by a thought, turned and hailed a passing droshky. It might be as well to go to the GPU and find out if there was anything in their records against one Sokolin, surgeon-dentist, and if he could not by any stretch of imagination be made to fit the missing "S", the writer of the mysterious note, and the unknown quantity in the "White Eagle".

Tretikov listened to the Procurator's story with attention, but with a certain ironic lift of his eyebrows that somehow made the narrator feel that perhaps he had been allowing a usually well-controlled imagination to run away with him.

"Do you know anything about any other of this lady's clients?" asked the official, after patiently hearing a full account of the other's observations and suspicions.

"Yes, one other," said Nikulin, somewhat dashed in his spirits to find that Tretikov was not impressed with the material about Sokolin to the exclusion of everything else. "A man I already know in connection with the case—Gorbunov, Ballet Manager at the Bolshoi. His connection with Pavlov, however, appears to have been exclusively theatrical, and he certainly does not give the impression of a man with political interests, though he seems an extremely reactionary type, like most of Madame Burova's clients."

"And this Sokolin strikes you as a man likely to have been mixed up in politics at one time or another?"

"That is perhaps more than I should like to say. But I am prepared to swear that he is a man with some sort of secret, living in constant fear of discovery. That's pretty plain, though *what* he is trying to hide is, of course, not clear."

"Well, it'll do no harm to look into the lives of both these gentlemen—I mean the ballet man as well," said Tretikov and the Procurator understood that the interview had come to an end.

He went away a little less impressed than he had been when he entered with his theory of Sokolin as an important factor in the Pavlov case, but by no means inclined to relinquish him altogether. All the way to the quiet restaurant at which he usually dined, and all through dinner, he turned over in his mind the features of the case as he knew them. One very strong point he considered to be the fact that the murder had been committed very skilfully, and this was a point against the surgeon-dentist, who might be supposed to be able to handle a knife as well as, or better than, another.

CHAPTER XVI

"THE WICKED FLEE
WHEN NO MAN PURSUETH"

A FEW HOURS later Nikulin received a visit from the faithful Yanovitsky, who had information which made the Procurator declare to himself triumphantly that wisdom had once again been justified of all her children, by which a man usually means that he has been right again. For it was important and significant information. It appeared that Yanovitsky had been passing the entrance of the GPU himself when Nikulin's droshky had drawn up to the door. This had naturally attracted his attention and he was just going up to speak to his chief when he happened to notice a droshky which drew up immediately behind the one from which the Procurator had alighted. He then observed that its occupant was leaning forward with his eyes almost starting out of his head and gazing after the Procurator's figure disappearing into the entry. Next moment the unknown man stopped the driver, evidently without any previous warning, for the droshky had not even begun to slow down. This strange behaviour made the prescient Yanovitsky suspect that the droshky had been instructed to follow Nikulin's, but that its occupant had not had the slightest idea whither he was following him. When the Procurator had disappeared altogether, the unknown had dismissed his own droshky at the corner and strolled over to the stopping place of the motor buses. Now this seemed somewhat peculiar to Inspector Yanovitsky, who could not understand what should make a man get off a droshky to stand and wait for a motor bus. He thought on the whole that he could scarcely do better than emulate the eccentric behaviour of the unknown, and watch developments.

"Why didn't you come in and warn me?" growled Nikulin.

"And lose sight of him while I was gone, as well as giving him a chance to identify me?" parried Yanovitsky sapiently.

"Well, what was he like? Go on!" said Nikulin.

He was a little sore at the failure of his sleuth-hound system to make an impression on Tretikov and was all unconsciously and most unfairly venting a little of his irritation on his subordinate.

"Stout, tall gent with a red face and pop eyes," said Yanovitsky. "And he stood there on the corner and let bus after bus pass by, but he never took his eyes off the entrance you had gone in by."

"Sokolin," said the Procurator to himself, "and as neat a way of watching a door as I ever heard of."

"We stood there three-quarters of an hour," continued Yanovitsky, "or almost that, and then you came out and my chap was over to the taxi stand in a moment, and pointing you out to the driver. It didn't take me long to get into a taxi behind him and point *him* out to the driver, and then you put us both in a fix by getting into a number 6 bus. But he was all right. He hopped into the seat beside the driver, and kept you in sight all down the Tverskaya and then again you led us a dance by going into a restaurant and keeping us waiting another three-quarters of an hour. I dismissed my taxi at once on the other side of the road, and went straight into the restaurant. It was very crowded, so instead of going to look for you, I took a seat by the door and kept a watch through the window on my gentleman. Evidently he wasn't hungry, or he was afraid of risking missing you if he went and ordered dinner, for he filled in the time in the street. He had his boots cleaned at the corner and then he went to a kiosk and took a long time buying a 'Pravda' and then he crossed over to another corner and brought cigarettes at another kiosk and then he just quietly took his place in the Information Bureau queue on the corner, you know, and kept letting people pass him, until he saw you come out. I let him get in front and then I followed on. You went on foot to your office, he followed. As soon as you went right in, he walked up the steps, examined the name plate, popped with his eyes till I thought they would fall out, and then went away, me after him."

Yanovitsky went on to describe how he had followed his man to Sand Street, identified him as C. I. Sokolin, Surgeon-Dentist, and come straight round to report to his chief.

The first thing to do was obviously to have Sokolin watched. Nikulin was pardonably elated at this additional proof of his penetration, and took immediate steps to have his sceptical friend at the GPU informed of it. After this he thought even the most sober-minded and bureaucratic officials could scarcely afford to ignore the importance of his researches. He received little more satisfaction over the telephone than a "Ha! Extremely interesting. You are having Sokolin watched, you say. Night and day? Very proper." But nothing could diminish the Procurator's feeling of elation and of being at last on the track of Pavlov's murderer.

The block of flats in Sand Street was watched back and front, and before turning in for the night the Procurator received the satisfactory report that Sokolin had been followed to the Art Theatre, where he had gone alone.

"Well, he's safe for a few hours," said the Procurator. "But keep a man in front of his house, and a couple at the theatre."

But the next morning Yanovitsky, extremely crestfallen, had to report a catastrophe: Sokolin had not returned from the theatre. The men stationed at the exits had somehow missed him in the crowd, or he had slipped through in disguise and those posted outside the flats were quite convinced that he had not returned home at any time during the night.

The Procurator looked at Yanovitsky as if he would like to bite him or do something equally savage to him. But it was no good. Sokolin had gone and it was now a question where to find him. Enquiries at the booking office and theatrical agencies were fruitless, and it was quite impossible to ascertain whether Sokolin had been alone at the theatre, or whether he had been there at all. Nikulin was inclined to think that he had merely joined the ingoing throng to throw dust in his pursuer's eyes, and then, without troubling even to go through the formality of taking off his hat and coat, had slipped out by another exit. There would have been no difficulty about this, as there is always a small but surging crowd coming and going in the endeavour to get in on the free list in all Moscow theatres. Nikulin now felt pretty sure that Sokolin had been thoroughly aware that he was under observation. The Procurator knew the degree of subtlety with which police employees are wont to watch a house, or shadow a suspect, and could imagine that not only the astute Sokolin, but probably all the inhabitants of the whole block, if not of the whole yard, knew within half an hour that the house was being watched. Stern questioning of the crestfallen sleuths elicited the interesting detail that Sokolin had come out of the front door, murmured: "Oh, my stick!", dashed back and reappeared with a stick almost immediately. The Procurator felt pretty sure that Sokolin had gone back to have a look at the back entrance. When he was informed that the man posted in the yard had ensconced himself comfortably on the lid of a sand-bin, in full view of the back staircase, Nikulin swore loud and long in his wrath.

The next thing was to visit the railway stations. The night express to Leningrad had been booked up two days in advance, but this by no means precluded the possibility of sudden flight by train, as a man of Sokolin's probable experience of the seamy side of life would always know how to get a ticket at a moment's notice through unofficial channels, and the men who made a business of such speculation were not the men to give away their clients.

So the Procurator was faced with the fact of Sokolin flown: either flown altogether from Moscow, or hiding in the purlieus of the city somewhere. At the other big stations no traces of a man of Sokolin's description—a big man in a black cloth overcoat with an astrakhan collar were to be found. The only outstanding feature of his appearance was the grey trilby hat which the watchers reported him to have been wearing on leaving his house and entering the theatre. As on the whole more caps are worn in Moscow than hats, especially when travelling, this was at least something to go by, though to be sure there was nothing to prevent Sokolin from discarding his hat by the way and exchanging it for a cap stuffed in his pocket. In fact the Procurator supposed that this was what he had actually done.

His suspicions were confirmed by the story of a cloakroom attendant who had noticed a hat on a shelf over the clothes pegs in the ground floor cloakroom, after practically the whole audience had left the theatre with their hats and coats. He had noticed the hat several times, because he kept expecting it to be claimed, and at last found himself giving away the last consignment of coats and goloshes while the hat remained there lonely. It had struck him as funny, because either someone must have forgotten his hat, in which case he would have returned for it as soon as he reached the door, or someone must have turned in a hat without a coat, and no one was likely to have come out on this bleak night without a coat, or been allowed to go into the theatre in one. Then he had been called to the other end of the cloakroom and when he came back the hat had disappeared. This was tantamount either to a confession of intended theft, or to an accusation of his colleague in the cloakroom. In any case the theatre was searched and the hat found lying behind a spittoon, and brought to the Procurator in his office.

He examined it curiously, thinking the while that he would himself have made a pretty good criminal, for Sokolin had done exactly what he would have done in his place: taken a cap in his pocket, quietly placed his hat on the shelf in the cloakroom, when the attendant's back was turned—to all appearances merely the act of an impatient man and provocative of no special attention, even if it should be noticed—and, turning away and losing himself in the crowd, quietly taken a cap out of his pocket and donned it.

There was at least a chance that anyone looking in a crowd for a man in a felt hat would be likely to overlook a man in a cap. Moreover, nobody had any special reason to look for a man five minutes after he had entered the theatre. The men had thought they were merely to report movements and did not know that they were shadowing a man already carefully planning flight, and this in a sense excused their carelessness in not keeping close to him, even in the theatre. So brilliantly successful had been the dentist's ruse.

The hat was an ordinary grey heavy-weight felt, with the mark of a government store stamped on the lining. The ribbon binding round the rim was beginning to fray at the right side, and the inside leather binding was stained irregularly with the familiar Alpine line of sweat. The hat only had its one secret and it delivered it up immediately: it told the Procurator that its owner had discarded it to provide himself with a temporary disguise. And that much he felt he had known beforehand. The hat looked as if it had been worn for more than one winter and a reference to the store at which it had been sold showed pretty conclusively that it had been bought three years ago, and there was, of course, not the slightest hope of retracing the purchaser. In any case, thought the Procurator ruefully, this would get us no further, for the hat was practically certainly Sokolin's and the fact of his being in flight was well-enough established.

CHAPTER XVII

BLIND ALLEY

NEVER DID A man appear to have covered up his traces as well as this man who had simply left his house to go to the theatre—and vanished. His rooms were, of course, carefully and throroughly searched, without any material results being produced. His history was elicited with little difficulty, and proved equally inconclusive. He had taken the full course for dental surgery in St. Petersburg before the war, and had practised as a dentist's assistant for two years in the suburbs of that town. The dentist for whom he had worked was dead and buried and the next few years of Sokolin's life were so far untraceable. An old khaki uniform hanging in a cupboard pointed to military service during the war, evidence corroborated by papers found in his desk, relating to two years of service in a sanitary corps on the western front, in the capacity of regimental dentist. Again a few years proved untraceable, but as these had been years of revolution and civil war, there was nothing particular in that. In fact there was nothing whatever to lend colour to the idea that Sokolin had ever been a member of any political society, but, Nikulin told himself, equally nothing to show that he had *not* been.

Patients turned up at intervals at Sokolin's rooms, but although each was carefully followed up not one gave the slightest loophole for suspicion. One thing was pretty certain: Sokolin must have a good sum of money at his disposal, for a man could hardly leave his house at a moment's notice, without, apparently, so much as packing up a change of linen, unless he had money in his purse. Nikulin longed to see the effect on Burova of the loss of yet another of her clients, but he was too much afraid that Sokolin might have managed to put her wise to his identity, to risk appearing in person. He kept her watched and visited by a woman, but could find nothing suspicious in the accounts of her behaviour. She prattled in her open-hearted way to her new client, who employed Nikulin's innocent subterfuge and had her nails seen to regularly once a week, so that if he had deprived her of one client in frightening away Sokolin, reflected the Procurator, he had at least done what he could in compensation, though he scarcely thought the exchange would have seemed a good one to Madame Burova, whom his agent reported to be a kind of cretin. "A typical blonde."

"I beg your pardon," said the Procurator mildly, unable to refrain from a significant glance at his assistant's smooth flaxen locks. "Do you want me to infer that blondes are usually or necessarily half-witted? Now, if I were asked to describe you, the first thing I should say would be that you are a typical blonde."

"So I am," she replied tartly. "But not the sort that gentlemen prefer."

Nor was she, and the Procurator hardly knew what to say, so he became very businesslike.

"Have you found out how many customers—clients—she has?"

"She has twelve regular ones who come every week, two of whom are men. And I have seen various women who came once only and one man. All of them have been traced and identified."

She handed a list to her chief. The three men were a well-known tenor, a film-producer and the conductor of a small but celebrated private orchestra. Nothing in any way suspicious attached to any of them.

Burova herself had been many times approached for the dentist's address, both by genuine patients, and employees of the police, but either she really did not know it, or she simulated exceeding well, and the Procurator was reluctant to employ direct methods of bringing pressure to bear upon her, first because he did not feel sure that she really knew anything, and secondly because he did not want prematurely to scare another bird into flight.

During these days of doubt the Procurator vacillated between an instinct to go to Siberia in the trail of Malinovsky and Milutin and an instinct not to lose sight of the flat in Sand Street. He could not help feeling that a man who had taken so little with him at a moment's notice had not gone far, or at least would be back again sooner or later, when things had blown over a little. Probably Sokolin was following the case in hiding somewhere and was only waiting for the trial of the murderer of Pavlov to reappear and resume his practice.

And then one day Nikulin's woman assistant came to him with interesting information. As she had approached the door of Sokolin's flat for her weekly treatment at the hands of the fair Burova, she had found a seedy-looking individual engaged in profound study of the brass plate. Moved by some impulse which she herself could hardly understand, she asked him if he knew whether the dentist had returned yet. The answer had been that, as the seedy-looking individual had been ringing for ten minutes and got no reply, it didn't look like it. And he had supplemented his remark by exclaiming: "And I don't suppose he'll be in a hurry about getting back neither. I always did say he'd get what was coming to him, and so he will."

Struck by this remark the woman had had the presence of mind to express her disgust at not finding the dentist and even asked the seedy-looking individual if he could recommend her another, which had gained her a look of profound contempt but no other reply.

She had then turned and gone downstairs, to make her interest in the dentist appear bona fide, but waited about in the street as inconspicuously as possible to see the seedy-looking individual come out, which he did practically on her heels. Only great skill (she said) had enabled her to remain in his wake unnoticed, but she had managed to follow him to a tenement house in a very low district. Further she had not liked to go for fear of discovery, but she felt sure she could easily identify him.

The Procurator cheered up. Here, at any rate, was someone who knew something about Sokolin, and knew moreover, that he had something "coming to him". He dispatched the woman forthwith to accompany Yanovitsky, whose appearance was sufficiently villainous to arouse no particular attention in the lowest of localities, in order that she might identify her find and enable the detective to keep him under observation. The next morning Yanovitsky had his report ready. The observation had not cost him much trouble, for he found he knew the man well by sight, as a petty malefactor by the name of Smirnov continually in and out of gaol for what the detective described as "small but low-class offences". The police records soon yielded information of four or five convictions during the last two years—

for being party to a transaction in cocaine, for acting middleman in the sale of smuggled silk stockings, for receiving goods systematically stolen over a long period by a gang of young thieves recently cleared up, and for taking money from a street-walker for the use of a room.

The Procurator had the man Smirnov brought before him, and the first impression made him feel that he was on the wrong tack: whatever this bit of flotsam and jetsam had against Sokolin, it was surely not murder! A little shrunken man, with a watery eye and walrus moustache: a narrow, pushed-in-face, a narrow squeezed-in chest: a tie like a piece of chewed string: a hand like the foot of a toad: a neck that might not have shamed a canvas bag, but was a poor thing to support a human head: patched and broken felt boots: a black coat, green with age and grey at the seams: a husky voice and a palsied tread: such was the poor fish that had got caught in the net of the law.

"What do you know about Sokolin?" was the Procurator's first question.

"Who says I know anything about him?" was the wearily defiant reply.

"We know you do," said his interlocutor quietly, "and you've known for a long time that he had something coming to him."

The fishy eye rolled and sank. It looked as if it would flash if it had not long forgotten how.

"Well, and if I do?"

"Then we should like to know as well."

"Which of course you don't know anything more than the babe unborn." (Heavy sarcasm enriched the poor husky voice.) "Well, anyhow, I haven't got nothing coming to me."

"No, you've had yours this month," said the Procurator. "Now please let me know what you know about Sokolin. You will have to stay here till you are prepared to do so, so you might as well begin."

"I haven't done nothing against the law. I only come to see if he was back again."

"What made him go?"

"Why, I reckon he got wind that you got wind of him."

"And what did you want him for?"

"He owed me some money."

"How much?"

"Five rubles."

"What for?"

"I did some fetching and carrying for him couple of months back."

"Why didn't you come for it before?" questioned the Procurator, purposely leaving the question of the nature of the fetching and carrying open for the moment.

"It's written in those books why I didn't," said the wastrel, jerking his head in the direction of the shelves behind the Procurator's head, apparently under the impression that they bore prison records. "I was away from home at the time."

It was true. The Procurator already knew that this man had come out of prison since Sokolin's disappearance.

"Well, now, what was this fetching and carrying, my good fellow? You know very well that you'll have to tell me in the end, so what's the use of hedging?"

"How do I know? I know I carried packets from one party to another party, but I don't know what was in them, do I?"

"So. You carried packets from Sokolin to another party and you don't know what was in them. Haven't the least idea, eh?"

"Not the least idea," was the stolid answer, but a fish-like gleam came to life in the watery eyes, that bespoke a sentinel pre-warned of danger.

Having at last by sheer persistence wrung out of the miserable creature the name and address of the party to whom he had carried packets from Sokolin, the Procurator dismissed him, but gave orders for him to be retained for the night in the district gaol. He could not feel that one night more or less in prison could mean much to such a man, and the philosophical shrug with which the order was heard proved that he had been right.

The name and address which the man had dictated at first conveyed nothing to the Procurator, but when he heard they belonged to a chemist with a flourishing business in the same district as that in which Sokolin lived, he thought he began to see daylight. Unhappily for him, however, the consequent illumination pointed away from murder and towards other and more familiar crimes against society. There was nothing in the least unnatural or suspicious in the fact of small packets passing between a chemist and a dentist in the same district. The only doubtful feature was the employment of so suspicious a character as Smirnov. The Procurator took up the telephone book, intending to find the chemist's number and ring him up, but then he remembered that this might be a man as easily put to flight as Sokolin had been, and decided to go himself.

It was drawing near to closing time. The shop was full of customers, mostly waiting patiently for medicines that had been ordered earlier in the day. Before approaching the counter the Procurator had a good look round. There were three people behind the counter—two men and a woman—all in white coats. Of the men, one had a head like a billiard-ball, smooth and polished, reflecting the light from the lamps, and a long black beard tinged with grey, as if he wanted to show that he could grow hair when he chose to. The other was a small, shifty-looking fellow with unpleasantly pointed ears. If the Procurator had been asked to point out the one more likely to be engaged in nefarious dealings of any sort he would undoubtedly have chosen the latter, but something proprietary in that black beard and vast, shaven skull, something august in the expression of their owner's features made him think that here was the boss and not the employee. Moreover, he reminded himself, criminals so seldom look the part. Fortified by these meditations he approached the larger man and said firmly: "Citizen Chernov, I must have a few words with you, if you please."

The guess had been right. A pair of steady watchful, grey eyes were raised to the Procurator's face.

"Perhaps you will be kind enough to wait twenty minutes. The shop will be closed and then I shall be at your service."

The voice was deep, magisterial, well-nigh priestly. Nikulin at once felt that its owner was a man of cultivation, who had assuredly not begun his career behind the counter.

"I'm sorry," said the Procurator, beginning to open his coat so as to produce some paper to show the fellow, "but my business won't wait."

Something in his voice, or was it the gesture towards his inside pocket, must have carried instant conviction. Without a word the great head was inclined with dignity, a flap in the counter opened under the Procurator's nose, and he was led through a glass door into the private sanctum behind the shop. It was at once evident that the small dark room was not used for living purposes. But of course, reflected the Procurator, it would have been naïve to expect Chernov to live here. Ground is too expensive in the centres of large cities to be used for the mere purposes of daily life. A naked electric globe exposed a table covered with papers and bottles. A typewriter with a dented cover stood on the floor and a black cat was curled up on the only chair. Chernov removed the cat from the chair and invited his visitor to sit down. The latter was not slow in coming to the point.

"What can you tell me about Sokolin?" he said, keeping his eyes fixed on the man's face. Nothing in the man before him betrayed shock, if any was felt, but the hands.

"Sokolin?"

The curved eyebrows darted up, wrinkling the immense forehead. One hand left the cat to go searching for cigarettes—or was it to gain a little time for thought? For the Procurator saw that cigarettes and matches were at hand on the table.

"Sokolin?" repeated the chemist, this time knitting his brows as if for reflection. "You won't smoke? You don't mind if I do?"

The little ceremony of striking a match, setting the cigarette alight, shaking the match and looking round for the ashtray before dropping the dead match into the wastepaper basket under the table occupied a few seconds.

"And who is Sokolin, if I may ask? The name is a common one, but I don't think—"

"Constantin Ivanovich," said the Procurator curtly, mentally registering another rapid blink of the small eyes.

It was as if, Nikulin thought, his words were felt by the man at his side like a fist shaken in his face, causing involuntary, inevitable flinching. Still the chemist maintained a blank, questioning countenance.

"Perhaps you will be a little more explicit," he said, "I'm afraid the name has no associations for me."

"Constantin Ivanovich Sokolin, dentist," said the Procurator, never taking his eyes off his man.

The large, bald face was lighted up with recognition.

"Ah, my dentist!" he exclaimed. "Why didn't you say so before? One meets so many men in the day's work, and one doesn't remember all their names. Yes, of course, I know Sokolin. Did you come to speak about him?"

"Yes. I should like you to tell me what you know about him."

"What I know about him? Well, that's not much."

The cigarette was placed on the grooved end of the ashtray (found easily enough when really wanted, noted the Procurator). Chernov, whimsical-eyed, cocked his head at his visitor.

"What *does* one know about one's dentist?" he said in bantering tones. "One knows if he runs his drill into one's gums. One knows if his fillings fall out into the soup. If neither of these things happens, one knows next to nothing and forgets that as soon as one's paid the bill. Happy is the dentist who has no history in the memory of his patients. I know Sokolin as an excellent dentist and feel sure he's a very good fellow—a very good fellow indeed."

"Why did he suddenly disappear?"

Chernov shrugged.

"Really," he said, "I'm afraid I can tell you nothing of my dentist's movements so long as they don't concern myself, and as for the last six months I have fortunately not required his services, I have never given a thought to the worthy Citizen Sokolin, and I had no idea that he had disappeared."

"No?" said the Procurator politely. "Then, perhaps you can gratify my curiosity on another point: what was in the packets sent to you now and then by Sokolin, through the man Smirnov?"

"I—don't—understand—you," gasped Chernov faintly, white to the lips.

"I—think—you—do," returned the Procurator steadily.

The two men stared at each other. Both recognised that the defences were down.

"Come!" rapped out the Procurator. "What was it, man? Cocaine?"

"No, platinum," said the other simply.

Now the Procurator understood all, and his house of cards with regard to the murderer of Pavlov fell rattling about his ears. Platinum, which is a government monopoly in Russia, is sold in small quantities at standardised prices to accredited dentists for use in fillings: every now and then a dentist will hoard up illegal accumulations of the precious metal and sell it at enormous profit to a speculator. Now he understood why Sokolin had been so anxious to find out who had recommended an unknown patient to him, why his suspicions had been so quickly aroused at finding out his patient's connection with the OGPU, and why he had resorted to instant flight.

Chapter XVIII

THE RETURN OF THE DENTIST

TRETIKOV WAS TOUCHED at his friend's profound depression over his failure, but could not refrain from pointing out that he himself had never been particularly impressed by the idea of Sokolin as the murderer of Pavlov and the only surviving member of the White Eagle.

"But 'S'," said Nikulin dolefully. "It fitted in so beautifully. Almost the only intimate of Pavlov that we had found, and his initial really being 'S'. And the note being about the theatre, of which they are both known devotees."

"Too beautifully," said the other. "Clues are seldom so obliging. But, come, there's no need to be so downhearted, man! After all, instead of one criminal you've run two to earth—or rather two and a half, if we count the man Smirnov, who has really been caught rather too often to make it much of a triumph. But this platinum business is really a scoop—at one fell blow we expose a dentist speculating in platinum and a receiver of illicit goods. That is really good work, you know."

Nikulin brightened a little, but his voice was still despondent.

"I would rather have discovered the murderer of Pavlov than all the defaulting dentists in Moscow—"

"It's an open question, however, who is more dangerous to society," interpolated the other, "a man who deprives it of a not particularly valuable life, or one who continues for years systematically undermining trade and the development of industry, thus affecting the lives of countless hundreds. If I could rid society of the speculators I would leave it to deal with the murderers itself."

"All very fine," grumbled Nikulin. "But we haven't even got Sokolin—only frightened him away."

"But we have got Chernov, and I don't think it'll be long now before we get the other chap. You only want to catch one of them, they always squeal sooner or later—think it'll get them more lenient treatment.

"But now about your murder. Have you any more clues to follow up?"

The Procurator sighed.

"I still keep Dolidzey and Dubinsky under observation," he said, "but I'm bound to say I no longer believe in their guilt. Of course this letter about Pavlov from Siberia may have acted as a powerful suggestion on my mind, but I can hardly entertain any idea now but that of some sort of political murder on the lines you once sketched. On the other hand it is early yet altogether to exclude the possibility of murder for robbery or from motives of revenge or jealousy—and here, so far, I have only turned up Dolidzey and Dubinsky."

"Have you thought again about the man Gorbunov?"

The Procurator admitted that he had altogether dismissed the ballet manager from his mind. Here he thought both motive and evidence were lacking.

"Evidence so far we have none," admitted the other, "but motive need not be sought. We have only to prove that Gorbunov was Milutin to have at least sufficient hypothetical motive."

"But why should he be?" objected the Procurator.

"And why should he not be?" parried Tretikov. "Listen to this."

He opened a drawer at his left hand and extracted a bundle of papers loosely kept together in a blue jacket.

"Gorbunov: Alexander Fedorovich," he read aloud. "Manager of Ballet Department in Grand Theatre since November, 1924. Before that organised Ballet Department in Bolshoï Theatre, Kiev. Previously to this had taken a theatrical touring company throughout Great Russia, beginning with Siberian towns. Birthplace given as Yablo, a small town three times taken and retaken by Whites and Reds, in which all registers and municipal documents were destroyed by fire."

He stopped reading, looking up from under his brows at the Procurator, without raising his head from the paper in his hand.

"Now, Comrade Nikulin," he said, "can you see anything inherently improbable in a man with such a record having belonged to a counter revolutionary band? All documentary evidence conveniently destroyed during the civil war—perfectly plausible and highly convenient, eh?"

"Well, I will have him watched," said the Procurator reluctantly.

"I shouldn't trouble to do that," said the other drily, "I have had him under close observation for at least a week without frightening him into flight. He hasn't the least idea that he is being watched."

The Procurator blushed.

A letter found among Chernov's papers showed that Tretikov had not been far wrong in thinking that Sokolin would soon be traced now that they had got his accomplice. The letter was unfinished (or perhaps it had been a draft), and unaddressed, but it began promisingly, to wit, *My dear Constantin Ivanovich! There is no "reason" why you should not come back immediately. I think you were mistaken in thinking the climate of Moscow unhealthy for you. Anyhow, I have been all right the whole time and it is highly likely that if there were anything going I should be the one to catch it first, having been the most subject to infection.*

I think I have discovered the secret of your mysterious patient. As a result of much patient digging in the mentality of your brilliant lady friend and manicurist I think I have discovered that it is a question of the murder of P. that Nikulin was after. Obviously there is therefore not the slightest reason why you should not come back and "resume your practice". I shall be very glad to see you, as I don't want to be forced to go to another dentist.

This letter seemed to the Procurator to make it perfectly clear, if any doubt still remained, that Sokolin had had nothing to do with the Pavlov murder. The allusion to resuming his practice and Chernov's reluctance to go to another dentist was obviously intended as a veiled threat that the platinum business would be carried on without Sokolin if he did not hurry back.

After this it was simple enough to wring from Chernov Sokolin's address. At first the chemist refused all knowledge of it, but was silenced by being confronted with his own letter, and finally furnished the address of a Crimean sanatorium where his accomplice had been recuperating his health under another name, waiting to hear from Chernov when the latter should consider the storm blown over.

C. I. Sokolin, surgeon-dentist, was surprised to be met at the station when he returned in a week from his holiday. And now, as far as the Pavlov murder was concerned, the Procurator saw him disappear from the scene. It was not without regret that he did so, for there was something about the burly rogue that interested him and he still thought he would have made the most suitable candidate for a political murder. Indeed, he was so far the only one of all the hares that had been started that impressed his pursuer as able to carry the thing off.

CHAPTER XIX

SILK STOCKINGS DO MATTER!

THE PROCESS OF elimination of possible murderers left Gorbunov high and dry. True he had done nothing to arouse suspicion and nothing could be found against him, but the fact remained that he was the only known acquaintance of the murdered man who had not as yet been counted out either by a suitable alibi or inherent improbability. Moreover, he also was, or had been, a client of Madame Burova, and the Procurator still felt that the key lay there somewhere. The convenience of the back staircase seemed to him to be too great to have been a mere coincidence.

It occurred to Nikulin that he had neglected one source of possible information with regard to Gorbunov—the girl Dolidzey. He remembered suddenly that the ballet manager when asking permission to see Tamara in prison had expressed his belief that the girl would be likely to speak freely to him "because she has confidence in me. She knows I am her friend", or something of that sort. What if Tamara should prove to be able to throw some sort of light on this enigmatic figure? The next day he sent a message to the theatre desiring that Dolidzey should visit him during the day. She arrived visibly scared, but otherwise looking so radiant and blooming that the Procurator could hardly take his eyes off her. She is like a dark incarnation of the spring itself, he thought to himself, or no, with her white teeth and black eyes she is like Minnehaha come to town. Which only shows that spring can get in through district police station windows, even if ultra-violet rays cannot.

"Now, you have nothing to look nervous about, Tamara," he said kindly, "for I'm not going to have you locked up again, or anything like that. I only want a little—er—assistance from you.

"I know you're a sensible girl and will try to understand what I'm going to say to you and keep it to yourself. And I hope you're not going to let any unpleasantness in the past, which no one regrets more than I, Tamara, prevent you from having confidence in me."

She shook back her short black mane and laughed so that a double row of strong white teeth was exposed to the Procurator's not indifferent gaze.

"*Now* what is it you want?" she said. "I never shall get used to this way of first saying a speech and then saying what you want. Tell me what you want to know, and if I can I'll tell you."

The Procurator was silent for a moment, regarding her over his folded arms. He hesitated, partly not having quite made out his mind as to how to approach the subject of Gorbunov, and partly because it was a pleasure to him to see her sitting there so young and fresh and confident.

"Have you made it up with Dubinsky, Tamara?" he said at last.

"Made it up with him? I never quarrelled with the foolish boy. I simply couldn't be bothered with him, and I still can't, that's all. With him or any of the rest of them," she added, half under her breath.

"Are there so many of them, Tamara?" inquired the Procurator.

His glance fell on her sturdy legs, crossed at the knee. Their shining surface made him reflect that Tamara must have decided that silk stockings after all *do* matter.

"I tell you, I don't know what's the matter with the men," said the girl confidentially. "I'm not pretty and I'm not anything special and I only want to get on with my work. You'd really think men couldn't bear to see a girl that has her heart in her career, and doesn't sit and think about them all day. I don't want anything from them, why can't they let me alone?"

"But who are these men who won't let you alone?" questioned the Procurator mildly.

"All of you," was the spirited retort. "I declare I thought even you were going to begin to-day!"

"I?" exclaimed the Procurator. "Now, my dear girl, what earthly right have I given you to say a thing like that?"

"I don't know," she said, eyeing him doubtfully. "I thought you looked at me very sentimentally just now."

He laughed outright.

"That's the spring, Tamara. We can't help that, you know."

"The spring!" she snorted. "How is it that the spring never worries me, I wonder?"

"It will, Tamara, it will," he assured her. "But come now, tell me what's the trouble. I promise not to make love to you."

"It all began with those two old men," she said in aggrieved tones.

"Which two old men?"

"Why, poor old Pavlov, of course, and Gorbunov."

The Procurator almost jumped in his chair.

"Gorbunov? What do you mean by that, Tamara? Surely Gorbunov has never made love to you?"

"Oh, of course not!" she responded disdainfully. "He wouldn't do such a thing, would he now? I don't know what you call making love, but I do know that he's pestered the life out of me ever since I've been fourteen years old, and if it weren't for him perhaps poor old Pavlov would be alive to-day, not that it matters in my opinion whether he's alive or dead," she added spitefully.

"But, my dear child, why did you never tell me any of this before?" said the Procurator. "Can't you see it was your duty?"

"My duty?" she faced him round-eyed. "What for?"

"Why, what have you just said? If it hadn't been for Gorbunov perhaps Pavlov would be alive to-day. What did you mean by that?"

"Oh, that!" she laughed easily. "I didn't mean anything special. I only meant that if it hadn't been for Gorbunov I should never have met Pavlov, and perhaps if Gorbunov hadn't been so cross about my going to Pavlov's rooms, I mightn't have been so determined to go. I'm like that, you know—very obstinate if I'm crossed."

"So it was Gorbunov who introduced you to Pavlov, and then he didn't want you to dance for Pavlov?"

"That's right. First he introduced me to him, and then I suppose he saw that the old ass was getting sentimental about me and got jealous or something disgusting."

"Now, Tamara, this is important. I must have the story from the very beginning. I can't think how it is I have failed to get it before. Why, you foolish child, you never even told me that Gorbunov introduced you to Pavlov!"

"You never asked me," she replied.

He shrugged his shoulders in exasperation.

"Great heavens, I asked you to tell me all you could remember about your relations with Pavlov and all you could tell me was that you met him at the Arts Club, at an after theatre supper. But you never told me Gorbunov was there."

"Well, he wasn't. Not with us, I mean. He came in afterwards alone and walked across and told me Pavlov wanted to know me."

"Ye gods! And I hear this now, for the first time!" exclaimed the maddened Procurator. "Well, now, at least, let's have it all. After this meeting how many times did you see Pavlov?"

"Once or twice at the Club—three times, perhaps. And once after the theatre."

"Was Gorbunov present on these occasions?"

"Sometimes he was, I know. For he told me afterwards that it wouldn't do me any good to get associated in people's minds with that type of man."

Yes, Nikulin remembered, the ballet manager had said something of the same sort to him, long ago.

"Yes," she mused, "and once he came up looking very black and said something to Pavlov that I didn't quite hear, but I heard him say: 'You'd better not,' or something of that sort."

"And what did Pavlov answer?"

"I don't think he did. He just smiled and shrugged his shoulders and went on talking to me."

"And what else can you remember between yourself and Gorbunov, regarding Pavlov?"

"That's about all, I think," said the girl, raising her eyeballs as people do when they want to try and recall something.

"And now you must tell me all about your relations with Gorbunov. How long is it since he's been making love to you?"

"You might say on and off for five or six years," said Tamara. "And worse after Pavlov got to know me."

Now what did she mean by making love, thought the Procurator.

"Do you mean he tried to kiss you and so forth," he said cautiously.

"Kiss me!" she echoed fiercely. "I'd like to see him or any man try, if I didn't want them to. No, but you know what I mean, always pestering and hankering."

And all his efforts could not get anything more definite out of her.

"Well, and now?" suggested the Procurator.

"Oh, lately, he's begun again. Especially since he's known he's going abroad—"

"Abroad?" echoed the Procurator. "Gorbunov is going abroad?"

"Yes, he's got a commission from the theatre to go to Paris. There's a choreographer there whose methods he has to study or something. I don't really know, I'm sure. But I do know it seems to have made him more sentimental than ever about me, and I'm about sick of it. And it makes it so difficult him being my chief, as you might say. But, thank goodness, he'll be away a whole month and I shall have a holiday."

Here was important testimony indeed—and all in support of Tretikov's suspicions. For here was evidence of intimacy—carefully concealed—between Gorbunov and the murdered man and an alternative to add to a possible political motive for murder, in the shape of jealousy, certainly not one of the least frequent causes for murder in the annals of crime.

CHAPTER XX

THEN, WHO WAS "S"?

THERE WAS NOTHING for it but to lay this fresh
information before Tretikov, who received it with commendable
reserve.

"Aha!" he said. "Very good! We're getting on, Nikulin,
getting on. The motives are coming on nicely, aren't they? And
as for evidence—"

Here it seemed as if he really could not keep a note of pardon-
able pride out of his voice. "I have stumbled upon a discovery
perhaps not less important than any that have been made."

He bent down to pull out a lower drawer in his desk from
which he drew with the utmost care, and something almost like
the reverence of a museum curator handling Greek antiquities, a
shallow, open tray.

"Here is something that may interest you. These objects were
found in a disused iron stove in Gorbunov's room. Interesting—
eh?"

Nikulin rose eagerly, and bent over the tray. It contained a few
minute charred scraps of something that looked like paper, a
little heap of something obviously softer and stickier, and—a
tinfoil coin with a hole pierced in it. It was this last which was
the object of the Procurator's immediate interest.

"In Gorbunov's room?" he gasped. "But I don't understand . . . How? . . . Have you arrested him?"

"Not yet. We're in no hurry."

He pointed with his pencil to the first little heap.

"Paper," he said, "and probably burnt, according to the opinion
of our chemical experts, any time from three weeks to a month
ago."

The pointing pencil moved on to the next heap.

"Rubber—burned at the same time—possibly the remains of
a thin rubber glove."

"And this—" the pencil moved on to the coin, "exhibit three

is the most interesting of all. And here *your* opinion, Comrade Procurator, may be considered expert. Have you—in the course of collecting evidence in the Pavlov murder—seen anything at all like this?"

The Procurator could hardly believe his eyes.

"Why, it's just like the missing coin from the bolero of Dolidzey's dress!" he exclaimed.

"We believe it to be not merely like, but the missing coin itself, but for obvious reasons I prefer to get hold of Gorbunov before rousing any suspicions by going to the theatre to verify this."

"It is—it almost undoubtedly is," said Nikulin. "But tell me, please, how it came to be in Gorbunov's room."

"I have a theory," said the other modestly, "but it may of course be fantastic. We shall see. Supposing Gorbunov to have entered Pavlov's house, using the back entrance of the flats, as we know he could perfectly well have done. Say he enters late at night, intending to make a desperate attempt to possess himself of, say, some document incriminating to himself, that he knows Pavlov to have. He comes with no specific criminal intent. But he takes a pair of rubber gloves with him. Just in case ... He finds Pavlov bending over his gramophone, on which he is just changing a record. Seeing himself unobserved, Gorbunov turns quietly to the writing table and the first thing to strike his eyes is the dagger, sticking in the top of it. Not for nothing has he dreamed o' nights of ways of getting rid of Pavlov—the only living being, mark you, who could bear witness to Gorbunov's past, the only man who could wreck his present. And now the dagger is, as it were, offered to his hand, and the unsuspecting Pavlov is offering his neck to the dagger. To seize the dagger, to plunge it into Pavlov's jugular, is the work of half a minute. Then a rapid search of the contents of the desk, the note-case is emptied and thrown on to the floor to make it look like a murder for theft. Then out again and home through Burova's flat, of which he has the key in his pocket. The papers and the gloves are stuffed hurriedly into the cold stove, a match put to them and the only existing documentary evidence as to the identity of Gorbunov with Milutin is destroyed. Next morning, Pavlov is found murdered, with the ballet girl Dolidzey's knife in his gullet, and his rifled note-case on the floor. Nothing to associate Gorbunov with the murder— no possible clue. And yet we have got him."

"And the sequin—the coin?"

"Oh, that! It may have fallen on to the desk during the struggle between Pavlov and Dolidzey, and either lodged itself in the fold of a letter, or stuck to the rubber glove. They're very sticky things, these tin coins, you know, with their sharp edges."

"And 'S'?" persisted the Procurator.

Tretikov smiled.

"Ah, I fear we shall have to renounce 'S'," he said. " I should have thought Mr. Sokolin would have given you a sickener of gentlemen whose names begin with 'S'."

The Procurator shook his head with a dissatisfied air.

"I should like to find 'S'," he said.

"Well, have a look for him," bantered the other. "He may turn out to be an utterer of forged notes, or the owner of an illicit still. He's pretty sure to be some sort of a bad hat, to judge by most of the late lamented Pavlov's pals, and that's always interesting and valuable. But I don't *think* you'll find him to have been the murderer of Pavlov."

The chagrin of the Procurator was horrid. It irked him badly to remember that Gorbunov had been brought to his notice at the very beginning of the case, that he had even harboured instinctive if vague distrust of this man. If it had not been that he had at first felt so certain of the guilt of Dolidzey, and later of Dubinsky and Sokolin, this distrust would certainly have inspired him to follow up more than one delicate and subtle suggestion from his own brain—hints which now stood out in such merciless black and white that is seemed to him he must have been a fool not to have deciphered them from the first. Had he not marked Gorbunov's extreme distress at the news of Dolidzey's arrest? Had he not noted the discrepancy between Gorbunov's denial of intimacy with the dead man and the fact of his obviously having borrowed from him literature of a shady nature—literature that, as he had told himself at the time, was scarcely likely to be exchanged with a mere formal acquaintance of the theatre? He remembered Gorbunov's obviously false explanation, at once involving Dolidzey and extenuating her crime. Had he not been long in possession of information proving that Gorbunov was free of Burova's flat and thence had access to Pavlov's house? As he tossed and turned on his uneasy couch he thought in his mortification that only the discovery of the identity of the mysterious "S" could restore to him some modicum of his self-respect. For was it not absurd that a man—an intimate friend of a murdered man, obviously in Moscow shortly before the murder and probably there still—should remain untraced? He had for long held that "S" might stand for Sokolin, and had continued in this belief until the finger-prints and handwriting, specimens of which had been taken immediately after his arrest, exploded this theory also.

When he had hastened to inform Tretikov of Tamara's startling information—that Gorbunov was going abroad—the official had smiled mysteriously.

"That's all right," he said. "He won't get any further than the frontier, of course."

"But why not arrest him immediately?"

"No hurry. In the first place the very fact, in the circumstances, of his attempting to leave the country will weaken any defence he may try to put up, and again, if he feels quite safe, as he obviously does, he may at the last moment risk communication with some other shady characters, and we may scoop up some more of them. The moment we arrest Gorbunov we put them all on their guard, let them think he is quietly leaving the country with our passport and they may get careless."

"Then you think there are some more of them. That Gorbunov is still politically active?"

"I don't, as a matter of fact," said Tretikov reflectively. "I believe the man cares for nothing but his own skin and would serve any master that paid him well, whether Soviet or Tsar, but he may possibly have associates. He is scarcely likely to be going abroad with the intention of returning to the U.S.S.R., and he may want to establish connections for the purpose of some form of speculation. You never know."

CHAPTER XXI

TAMARA TO THE RESCUE

LONG AGO, IN the almost mythical years before Russia was ravaged by civil war and foreign intervention, the District Procurator had been a married man. He had lived exactly a year with his wife, when they parted, never to meet again. This unimportant episode would have seemed to pass without leaving any traces on Nikulin's life, but for the fact that, somewhere in the South of Russia, a youth was growing into manhood who, though his infant lips had never called the Procurator or anyone else "Father", nevertheless cost that gentleman a substantial proportion of his monthly earnings. Nikulin took not the slightest interest in this young man, and if he occasionally remembered him on pay-day it was rather to wonder if it would not soon be time to stop this drain on his income, than to indulge his paternal instincts. He consulted a calendar on the day after his depressing night, and discovered that the child of his loins should have reached the age of twenty-one by Christmas. It was no doubt the momentarily depressed state of his mind that reminded him of his family obligations. Was it not time, he asked himself, for the youth to be independent of his unfortunate father? The Procurator shuddered to think that his son might choose a legal career, remembering the length of time he had been substantially dependent on his father, even after, nay long after, he had qualified as a lawyer. He seemed to remember hearing that his son aspired to be a civil engineer and thought, dismally enough, that this was possibly little better, since a young man brought up to believe in a permanent background of prosperity from a practically impersonal source, was scarcely likely to be in a hurry to become self-supporting.

Some obscure association of ideas made him cross over to his shaving-glass and perform heroic attempts to see the top of his own head. It didn't come off, but his prescient fingers told him, as plainly as a glass could have done, that there was a shining spot there about the size of a silver ruble. He sighed, stared at himself in the glass with hostility and then alarm—the face in the round mirror looking back at him seemed revolting, bloated: the skin was coarse and lustreless, the eyebrows sprouting horns like an old man's, deep crows' feet running from the corners of the bloodshot eyes to the hollowing temples. Strange he should never before have noticed what a singularly ugly man he was! He felt like Red Riding Hood surveying the once familiar face of her grandmother in dismay: oh, Grandmother, what long teeth you have! He had never considered himself a handsome man, at the zenith of his attractions, but neither had he thought himself a monster . . . Suddenly he noticed that the glass had revolved and that he had had a close-up of himself in the magnifying side. A twist of the screw showed him a very different picture—a refined face, showing, it is true, the traces of weariness around the eyes, but the sort of face that a man needn't be ashamed of: in fact the sort of face men did have. If it were not for that confounded bald spot . . . He sighed, took a cigarette and relapsed into his favourite armchair to read the papers. For some reason his eyes sought the theatrical announcements, though he seldom had occasion to consult them. Ha! Bolshoï Theatre! 7.30. "The Horse Hunchback". It was half-past six. The evening stretched ahead. Why not? In fact he had never seen her dance. In fact he was a middle-aged fool and she would soon have a right to say he was pestering her. But, hang it all, anybody could go to the theatre! She ought to be only too glad . . . That's what she danced for, to have people come to see her, when all's said and done . . . He put on his hat and went out.

The theatre was full and he could only get an absurdly expensive seat—in the second row of the stalls—right on the central gangway. Anybody peeping through the curtain from the stage might recognise him. They did peep through sometimes, the stage folk, to give themselves confidence by a sight of the house. He knew that. They had special little holes bored through the curtain for that purpose. A middle-aged fool . . .

In the third act, when the picture-beauties come alive and perform a delighted dance around the bewildered Ivan, who has called them into life by cracking his magic whip, the Procurator thought the whole audience must be looking at, thinking of, or whispering about Tamara, so did she seem to him to stand out.

In truth her clean action and rhythmic, spirited motions were already beginning to draw public attention to her, and Nikulin had the gratification of hearing her name mentioned with approval during the applause always rendered to this, one of the favourite dances in a popular ballet.

During the interval he fought with an inclination to go to the wings, decided that that might be interpreted as hankering, if not pestering, and turned resolutely towards the foyer, in which dense crowds were already revolving. The interval is one of the features of the Russian theatre. There are always two, if not three, and at least one of them lasts not less than thirty minutes. Nobody seems to mind a bit, and the whole audience pours into the corridors and foyer, and revolves perpetually, keeping with the utmost docility to the right, until three bells have been rung to warn of the beginning of the next act. Nobody takes any notice whatever of the first, at the second, couples say to each other: "Is that the first or the second?" but when the third peals out a general dash is made for the entrances, resulting in a block and ghostly figures crowding into their seats just as the curtain is going up.

Caught in the rhythm of this perpetual motion the Procurator, after having twice mechanically circled the foyer, suddenly caught sight of a familiar figure, with a small body and a large head, and a roving but sympathetic eye. At the same time Itkin, for it was none other than Julius Cæsarovich, caught sight of the Procurator, and stepped out of the crowd when he got to a corner, so that he could stop his friend when he in his turn should be carried by the revolving throng to the same spot. The two men were somehow unduly glad to see one another. Suddenly the first bell rang.

"Which one was it?" asked Nikulin.

"The first," said Itkin. "But it doesn't matter—don't let's go back. She isn't—I mean the last two acts are long and dull."

"Right," agreed the Procurator, whose interest in the ballet had suddenly evaporated, and who was delighted at being released from his solitary stall and with the prospect of company for the evening. "Let's go home and get a drink."

They walked the short distance to Nikulin's room, which was in an old house in a quiet street. There was no one at home, as Nikulin's charwoman was a daily, so he pulled the blind, put the electric kettle on to boil and set out all that his bachelor store-cupboard could provide—oranges, Albert biscuits, a packet of milk chocolate, a tin of anchovies and a half bottle of vodka. While he was thus occupied Itkin, who had been peering at his face in the mirror, placed inconveniently high for his small stature, or for that matter for anybody's, for the Procurator followed the curious principle adopted by so many people, of hanging mirrors above the level of the head and pictures above the level of the eyes, suddenly exclaimed:

"I say, Nikulin, tell me the truth, that's a good fellow—am I an exceptionally ugly sort of man?"

"Yes, Itkin," replied Nikulin absently.

He set a cup and saucer and a glass—his only attempt at a tea service—on the round table.

"Would you say I was going bald?" he said presently, pouring out the tea.

"Yes, Nikulin," said the newspaper man.

They drank their tea in melancholy silence, first broken by Itkin.

"And being so short makes it worse, of course," he said. "Some women *like* ugly men—prefer them—but they can't stand them as short in the leg as I am."

Nikulin silently pushed the vodka bottle over to him.

"I began to go bald when I was quite a young man," he said mournfully. "It didn't matter so much then, but at forty-five it's ageing."

Itkin pushed the bottle of vodka back. Neither touched it, they drank boiling hot tea and munched chocolate and biscuits and somehow felt comforted by each other's despondency. Neither of them mentioned Tamara, but when, after about an hour Itkin rose to go, each felt that confidences had been silently exchanged.

After the departure of Julius Cæsarovich the Procurator changed quite cheerfully into a gown and slippers, and settled down in his armchair to read a pile of journals that had long waited such a moment of leisure. To his surprise, however, he had hardly been settled in his chair five minutes before the door bell rang. Thinking it must be Itkin come back for something, he rose and went to the door. The light in the passage refused to respond to his finger and he remembered that the lamp had fused the day before. Opening the door and focusing his eyes about where Itkin's head ought to be, he found himself looking at a very healthy-looking coat button Letting his glance travel upwards, it came to a bearded face under a peaked cap which, in the dim light from the staircase, he did not at first recognise

"District Procurator Nikulin?" said a voice that was undoubtedly familiar.

"Yes, that's me," he said, still holding the door handle and looking uncertainly at the figure blocking up the doorway. The man took off his cap and then Nikulin realised at once that it was Gorbunov. Despite his astonishment, he had the curious feeling of having expected the man as soon as he saw him.

"Oh, come in, Citizen Gorbunov!" he cried, trying to conceal his surprise. "Very glad to see you."

Which he certainly was, but even more astonished. He apologised for the dark passage as he let his visitor in, and shut the door behind him.

"It's beautifully light in my room," he said reassuringly, assisting the stout man to remove his coat in the dark.

"First I must apologise for my intrusion at this late hour," said Gorbunov, settling his bulk into the armchair that Nikulin indicated. "I won't keep you above ten minutes, I assure you. My excuse is threefold. In the first place, I'm going abroad to-morrow."

The Procurator looked at his visitor curiously. Something in the man's face struck him as strange, and not quite as he remembered him. He would have said, if asked, that Gorbunov was of pale complexion, but now his face and eyes seemed to be suffused with blood. He wondered if he had been drinking. His speech was pompous as usual, but perhaps suspiciously careful.

"And in the second place," continued the complacent voice, "I saw you at the theatre to-night and that at the same time reminded me of you, and made me think I should find you still up. Indeed, I see I have not been your only visitor," he said suddenly, glancing at the table.

"Yes," said Nikulin absently. "A friend came back with me from the theatre—"

"Ah, yes, a short gentleman. I almost ran him down, I'm afraid, as I came up your stairs. And yet I think you were alone at the theatre?"

Not seeing any reason why he should be catechised, the Procurator favoured his visitor with a politely blank look.

"Well, as I was saying, I am leaving for Paris to-morrow, and very much desired to have a last little chat with you. I should like to know your opinion as to my two young charges, Dolidzey and Dubinsky? In your opinion, has all suspicion been entirely removed from them?"

"They are still under close observation," replied the Procurator cautiously.

"Ah, yes, that of course, officially. No doubt. For so long as no suspicion attaches to anyone else you are no doubt bound to consider them potentially guilty."

"Quite so," said the Procurator blankly.

"I should like to go abroad feeling quite free in my mind about these two young people who are, so to speak, under my care."

He took out a cigarette and lit it absent-mindedly and the watcher was not slow to note an unsteady hand. The Procurator kept turning over in his mind motives that should make a man take this risk just on the eve, as he doubtless thought, of getting clear away. Could it be that, after all, Gorbunov had had his suspicions aroused, and was feeling his way to see if they were justified? Or was he acting at the behest of an ill conscience? The Procurator knew how a bad conscience can ride a man in all manner of uneasy ways, making him refuse to leave well alone. Every key must be turned and turned again, even if the very act is suspicious: the creaking board must be traversed again, though doing so involves fresh risks, for there is no rest for the wicked.

"Yes," continued Gorbunov, his eyes on the Procurator. "I saw you in the theatre. It was Tamara who saw you first, before the curtain went up, and I saw you just before you went out during the interval."

"Really?" said the Procurator politely, wondering where all this was leading to.

Had the man come here after midnight merely to utter such commonplaces? Was this a case of feeling the aching tooth with the tongue whenever it stops throbbing? He wondered if Gorbunov had something on his mind which he could not bring out—some confession to make. That would be a scoop and one up against Tretikov. His eyes brightened at the thought and suddenly he caught Gorbunov's eye fixed on himself with a peculiar glint in it.

"I won't force him. I'll let him come to it gradually," he thought.

"Curiously enough," he said aloud in a conversational tone, "I was just wondering to-day if the audience can be seen from the stage."

"Yes, Tamara saw you," continued Gorbunov, almost as if he were continuing some line of thought of his own and had not heard Nikulin. "And I saw her looking and I came behind her, and looked and I saw you too. And I asked Tamara if she knew your address and she said she didn't, but it was probably in the telephone book and we looked and I found it and then I thought I'd come to see you!"

The subtle strangeness of the man's manner of speaking and especially the disquieting glint in his eye, grew more and more upon the Procurator. The conviction gained ground in his mind that the man had been drinking, perhaps celebrating what he regarded as his last night in the theatre.

"Well, I'm very glad you did," he said heartily. "Is there anything special you would like to say to me, before you leave?"

"Yes, there is," said Gorbunov, leaning forward, his whole manner changing so suddenly that for a moment the Procurator was quite startled.

"Now it's coming," he thought.

"There is," repeated Gorbunov harshly. "I want to know why the hell you've been making your fellows ring up Burova day after day, inquiring about me? Hey? What do you mean by it? That's what I came here to say."

"Ringing up Burova?" repeated the Procurator in genuine bewilderment.

Gorbunov suddenly sprang to his feet and whipped a revolver out of his pocket.

"Dog!" he screamed. "Dog! I'll shoot you down like a dog."

It is not at all comfortable to be at close quarters with an angry gentleman who has his revolver under your jaw and may be merely drunk, or may be murderous. The Procurator did not appreciate the situation at all, despite its novelty for him. He kept as still as he possibly could, being very solicitous that no motion of his own should precipitate affairs.

"Put that gun down!" he shouted. "You fool, it won't do you any good to kill me! We've got you anyhow, and there's no escape for you. You can only make matters worse for yourself."

"I'll make them worse for you first," said Gorbunov thickly, with a terrifying lurch of his gun hand.

The Procurator could now see that the man was completely drunk, and was astonished that he had not noticed it before. The crisis had brought it out suddenly, he supposed.

"It'll do me a lot of good to take me with you when I go. I'm going to kill myself first, then you."

"You'll find it hard to do that," said the Procurator grimly, "but I don't mind you trying a bit."

"I mean first I'll kill you and then myself," corrected Gorbunov with dignity, and suddenly pulled the trigger.

Nikulin saw a blinding flash and felt a violent concussion before he went down into darkness. The next thing he knew he was lying on his sofa, with Tamara's face bending over him.

"Why, he hasn't even been scratched!" he heard her voice in joyful surprise.

"Scratched?" he said. "Am I not dead then?"

Tamara's peal of laughter was joined in by a deep chuckle from the other end of the room.

At that moment a long ring was heard from the passage and Tamara ran to open the door.

The Procurator, suddenly regaining full consciousness, lifted his eyes to see two of his own familiar officers entering, heavy booted and with a clink of handcuffs, which they laid on the table, and followed by the faithful Yanovitsky, an expression of concern on his broad face.

"Here you are," came Itkin's voice. "I've had a job to hold him. For goodness sake, take charge."

The Procurator, turning, saw that the little man was pressing with all his weight on an overturned armchair, from underneath which, jutted a pair of trousers, finished off by elegant kid-top boots. The smiling officers stepped across, turned the chair right end up and exposed Gorbunov, his hair badly rumpled, his shirt sticking out over his waistcoat in front, and one arm out of his coat sleeve. He remained perfectly still, making no remonstrance as the men stooped down to fasten the handcuffs on his plump wrists and, one on each side, pulled him up into a standing position. At once, however, as if overcome with weakness, he sank into the chair beside him, and they let him be.

"Now will somebody explain to me?" said the Procurator mildly. "How is it you are here, Tamara? And you, Itkin—it seems to me that you bade me a fond farewell hours and hours ago."

The journalist cocked up his elbow to bring his wrist-watch within focus of his short-sighted eyes:

"Exactly three-quarters of an hour ago," he said, with a grin. The Procurator looked bewildered.

"Perhaps somebody will explain," he said weakly.

"You, Tamara," said Itkin.

The police officers and Yanovitsky assumed listening attitudes, and Nikulin, removing his legs from the sofa on which they had been stretched, sat upright and prepared to hear the story. Only the manacled man in the armchair paid no attention to her narration: he had a withdrawn, indifferent look, as if he were sitting in a railway waiting-room surrounded by strangers whose conversation could not be of the slightest interest to him.

"Well," said Tamara, "it was like this. Just before the second act I was peeping through on to the stalls, when I saw you. So I called out to one of the girls: 'Come and look! Here's Nikulin come to see me! Hope he doesn't want me for anything again.' ("I don't mean to say I wasn't very glad to see you," she added in polite parenthesis to Nikulin, "Only it always makes me a bit nervous to see you, you know.") Well, and just then I saw Gorbunov was just behind me. Without saying anything he went and put his eye to the hole and he had a very snarly look that I didn't like at all. But still I didn't think any more of it, only I did notice that directly after the act was over he rushed down to the theatre and had a look at you from the Director's box. I could see him from the wings and he was muttering to himself and looked very black. But what I didn't like at all was that just before the end he came to me very smooth and smiley and said: 'Tamara, I suppose you don't happen to know your friend Nikulin's home address. I shouldn't like to leave Moscow without saying a word of farewell to him. He's been very decent about this whole affair, you know.' Well, of course, I didn't know and I told him so. And somehow I didn't like the look of his face, and I thought he smelt very strongly of vodka, only I didn't think much of that at the time. I remembered it afterwards. And then as I was going out I saw him in the telephone box, not talking but looking in the book and then he shut the book and came out without using the phone at all. So I thought to myself: 'I bet he's been looking up Nikulin's address, now what does he want with my Procurator—nothing good, I'll be bound, besides I'm almost sure he's been drinking.' So of course I slipped into the telephone box after him and looked up your address myself and thought I'd just see if Gorbunov hadn't gone to see you and what for. And of course by the time I had my paint off and got changed he was gone and out of sight, so I thought I would take a taxi, only as it happened I had only seventy-five kopeks with me and of course that wasn't enough. But that's what I like about a life of crime," said Tamara earnestly, "it seems to purge you of all petty instincts. Now if it hadn't been for all this Sherlock Holmes business I shouldn't have even thought about taking a taxi, even if I'd had the money with me. But this time I wouldn't have thought twice about it, only of course I didn't have the money with me so it was no good my rising above the petty self of every day."

She paused to take breath and none of the men took their eyes off her animated face, as she sat facing them all, perched on the corner of the table, one sturdy leg swinging.

"Yes, well, since I couldn't take a taxi, of course, the next best thing was to get on to a tram, so that's what I did, and just as I was getting off at your corner whom should I see but Itkin waiting for the tram. So I thought that was rather a coincidence, and I went right up to him. And it was a long time before I could get him to listen to any sense, for he behaved in a most foolish way (Yes, you did, Itkin, and it's no good making faces at me, because I've got to tell this story in my own way, or I shall never get to the point!), and kept on gaping at me and saying: 'Tamara, it's too wonderful meeting you like this,' but at last I made him realise that the Procurator might be in need of a little sleuth-hounding, and then he came along with me double quick. And, as you know, it's a good ten minutes from the tram to your house and, of course, as ill-luck would have it, there wasn't a droshky to be seen—let alone a taxi, so we had to bustle along as best we could on our legs. And we were going up the stairs and I said to Itkin: 'How're we going to get in? For if Gorbunov means mischief, as I think he does, he's not going to answer the bell, nor let Nikulin either.' And then I had the inspiration to try and get in by the back entrance. And Itkin said, 'Supposing it's locked?' But I said: 'It may not be: people often only go round locking up just before going to bed.' And as it happened I was right and we got in through the kitchen and just as we got into the kitchen, I heard Gorbunov's voice shouting 'Dog!' or something rude like that, and next minute there was a shot and I rushed into the passage and found the door and when I came in you were lying half on the sofa, half on the floor and Gorbunov was standing over you with his head down and staring in a dazed sort of way at a smoking revolver in his hand. And that's all. Oh, yes, and then Itkin knocked Gorbunov down, and got the armchair on top of him and told me to telephone for Yanovitsky and an escort, and I did. And we were sure the Procurator was killed, but when I went to him I found he wasn't even scratched, only his ear was scorched, and the bullet had gone into the sofa, just half an inch from his neck."

The Procurator touched his neck just under his ear feelingly.

"Well, Tamara, you're a brick," he said.

"And so say all of us," said Itkin with conviction.

Yanovitsky cleared his throat as if he were going to speak, but only coughed instead and grinned across at Tamara.

"Well, the next thing is to get Mr. Gorbunov comfortable for the night," said the Procurator briskly. "We were expecting him to-morrow, but I think his room will be all ready for him. Yanovitsky, you go right down and get a couple of droshkies or a taxi or something."

Yanovitsky informed him that the police motor was waiting below and a spare taxi. Writing out a few brief instructions, the Procurator handed them to Yanovitsky, and in a few moments the detective, with the help of the escort, had invested the passive prisoner in his greatcoat and half led, half bore him out of the flat. He had not uttered a single word since the Procurator had returned to consciousness, and did not utter a word now.

Tamara was left alone with her two friends.

"Well, it's time for me to be getting along," she said, descending from her perch on the corner of the table. "Good night, Procurator."

She stretched out a lean, brown hand, which he clasped with emotion.

"Good night, Tamara," he said, "I have to thank you for my life to-night."

"You're welcome, I'm sure," she said with sober heartiness.

"He says I'm an ugly fellow," said Itkin, winding his scarf round his neck as the Procurator was helping Tamara on with her short coat. "Is it true, Tamara?"

"Goodness me!" cried Tamara impatiently. "What on earth does it matter? Look at me! Aren't I ugly? And yet everybody loves me."

"Do you really consider that I'm going bald, Tamara?" asked the Procurator. "Look me straight in the eyes and tell me if you consider me a very old sort of fellow."

"You are both darlings," said Tamara. And going from one to the other she implanted a hearty kiss on their cheeks, her arms flung round their necks in a proper bear's hug.

Which was not at all what they had meant.

Chapter XXII

BUTTON, BUTTON...

WHAT WITH FATIGUE, drink and who knows what terror, Gorbunov slept throughout the whole of the next day and when he awoke seemed in a curious torpor and unable to answer questions.

Puzzled by his allusions to Burova the night before, the Procurator decided upon a third interview with that houri, but this time thought she might come to him. Her astonishment at recognising him was comical, but she seemed not particularly perturbed at being sent for. She answered all questions readily. Gorbunov, it appeared, had been with her on the day before and he had been very nice—particularly so.

"I supposed it was because he wasn't going to see me for such a long time," she said naïvely, "but really he was so nice he was like another man."

"Was he usually not nice?" inquired the Procurator.

She flung up her hands.

"Oh, well, you know what the artistic temperament is," she said confidingly. "Always up in the heights or down in the depths, aren't they? I'm sure I'm like that myself. Well, but I hadn't seen Sasha for three weeks or more it would be. No, let me see it's exactly six weeks since he put foot inside my threshold. And you can't call that nice, can you? Anyhow, not matey. I felt it, I can assure you."

"Did you call him Sasha?" said the Procurator, bending forward in great excitement.

"Of course I did. We were great friends. Very intimate we were, and his name was Alexander."

The Procurator was searching hurriedly in his desk. At last he found what he wanted.

"Would this be Gorbunov's writing, d'you think?" he asked, holding out a half-sheet of notepaper for the lady's inspection.

"That's right," she said carelessly. "He always signed himself 'S' with his intimates."

And so Mr. S. was discovered at last. The Procurator felt profound disappointment, for his darling clue had led to no startling discovery. At the same time it was good to have even such a minor mystery cleared up.

"You're convinced it is his handwriting?" he said, pressing her.

"Well, I'm sure I ought to know if anyone," she said, a shade huffily, "seeing as I have an almost identical communication in my handbag."

She handed the Procurator a letter across the desk. It was a short note with reference to theatre tickets and also signed "S". A comparison of the notes pointed to their having been written by the same hand.

"Excuse me for interrupting you," he said politely, "you were going to tell me about your last interview with Mr. Gorbunov."

"Oh, yes, so I was," she said, settling comfortably into her chair, and evidently delighted with the opportunity to talk her fill. "Yes, so as I was saying he was so nice, bringing me flowers and chocolate and promising me a new dress because I was so upset."

"Why were you upset? Because your friend was leaving you?"

She opened her blue eyes wide.

"Oh, no," she said, "I've got too much character to get myself worked up about a thing that can't be helped. I always say I'm a bit of a philosopher and really, you know, gentlemen are very much alike in the end. They're very nice I'm sure and I should be the last to complain, because I'm sure the kindnesses I've received from gentlemen is unknown, and nobody can say the same of girls. But I mean that wasn't at all what I was upset about. It was about a dress I had just had back from the dressmakers, and there was a lovely button just on the left hip. I mean it wasn't exactly a dress, but more what you might call a négligé, blue crêpe georgette with a broad hem of heavy satin stitched on, and a beautiful black button on the left hip. I mean it really was a lovely button and I found it quite as you may say by chance, when I was looking through a lot of pins and odds and ends and it was the making of the dress, it was really. And can you believe it that dressmaker had gone and ruined it all by making the buttonhole too small! And you know what it is to make a buttonhole in crêpe de chine! I mean it's practically impossible and besides you don't go paying seven rubles to sit up at night sewing buttonholes yourself, do you? So of course he could see I was upset—I mean I was quite worked up. And he said don't worry about a thing like that on my last day girlie, I'll send you a new dress from Paris. So I said that's all very fine but as is well known the duty on silk articles is prohibitive. So he said he would get me one here before he left, and I must say he was very nice until I told him about the gentlemen who had kept on ringing me up about him all the week. Then he seemed to get queer all of a sudden and he went to the sideboard and had a drink and looked out of the window and asked me if I'd noticed the man with his collar turned up walking up and down the road before, and I said I certainly had, for he came every day and everybody in the house had noticed and wondered who was wanted, but as I had nothing whatsoever on my conscience I didn't take that much notice. So then he said he'd go out by the back staircase and I said: 'and what about my poor button?' and he was very rude and knocked it out of my hand through the window. Oh, I didn't tell you I'd cut it off the dress to see what I could do with it. And then off he went without so much as a look at me. And I looked everywhere for the button in the street, and at last I found it, but it was broken right in two, clean in two, so I suppose it really wasn't pure jet, but glass or something. But I was very upset all the same, because I had taken a fancy to that button. I'm very funny like that. Sometimes I take a fancy to things and then I'm awful, I don't seem to like to part with them."

She would have gone on in this strain for another half hour if the Procurator had not stopped her to put some salient questions. At first she refused to admit that Gorbunov might have left her flat at a late hour after midnight, but steady cross-examination produced a coy admission.

"Nobody thinks anything of that sort of thing nowadays, especially in the theatrical world," she said pompously. "You might almost say their day begins when other people's ends."

She seemed to have forgotten her pious strictures on Tamara's conduct in visiting a man's room at night.

It was obvious that she really could not make the effort to remember when Gorbunov had last left her so late, but it was clear that since the murder he had not done so once.

Feeling that he had for the present got all he required from this helpful lady, Nikulin dismissed her.

When Gorbunov was fit for cross-examination he showed himself to be a man of great resource and cunning. He did not attempt to deny that he had murdered Pavlov, and stated voluntarily that he had always known him to be Malinovsky, a former member of the notorious "White Eagle".

"I first came into contact with him when I was touring Siberia with a theatrical company," he said, "and recognised him at once when I met him in Moscow. I considered it a public duty to get rid of the man. Had Tamara been convicted I should at once have confessed, but I felt sure she would not be, and I was afraid my motives might not be appreciated, so I deemed it best to keep silence. The object of my visit to the Procurator was to find out if there was any danger of Tamara being punished for my deed during my absence. The regrettable sequel I can only attribute to my having drunk too much, and not knowing what I was doing."

Without waiting for cross-examination, he gave a full and voluntary description of the night of the murder, which appeared to Nikulin to be in the main truthful, and which tallied closely with Tretikov's theory of the crime.

"Happening to leave a friend's flat in the same yard," said Gorbunov, "I passed Pavlov's house. I went out by the back staircase, as it was nearer for me to go through the yard and out into Little Paul Street than to use the Sand Street entrance. Seeing a light in Pavlov's room, I decided to go up and see if Tamara had left him. I had known of her visit to him and disapproved of it highly, not thinking it a good connection for a young girl at the outset of her career. The side door leading to Pavlov's room was not locked, so I thought she was probably still there. On reaching the top of the stairs I saw that the door was ajar, and pushed it open without knocking. I thought I might catch them unawares. To my surprise, however, Pavlov was alone, with his head turned away from the door, absorbed in his gramophone. My glance fell on the dagger, quivering on the top of the bureau. It had a fatal fascination for me. I knew at once that it must be Tamara's dagger. It suggested to me struggle, violence, rape. I felt my breath come shorter. I seized the dagger and almost automatically stepped lightly across to the unconscious man and plunged it in his neck. I scarcely asked myself why, but when I saw what I had done, I said to myself, with a feeling akin to satisfaction: 'Another worm less on the earth!' I felt, and I still feel, that I have done a good deed in getting rid of this idle sensualist, this seducer of honest young girls, this counter-revolutionary. For who knows in what fresh intrigues and plots he may not have been involved. But naturally I could scarcely hope to convince others of the purity of my motives, and my next care was to cover my traces. His pocket-book lay open on the edge of the table. It was instinctive to empty it of its contents, to make the whole affair look like murder for robbery. And the next thing was to get away unobserved as quickly as possible. It would have been no difficult matter to get by the sleeping watch-man, but then I might have been observed and remembered at this early hour of the morning, in the street. I preferred the alternative of returning through the flat which I had just left, and of which, as it happened, I had the key of the back door in my pocket. I returned to my friend's flat, lay down on the divan without waking anybody, and the next morning at eleven o'clock, when the streets were full of passers-by, so that a man was no longer conspicuous, I went home at my leisure. My conscience was, and is, clean. I have rid society of one of its pests. That an innocent person should not suffer was my next concern, but I felt sure Tamara could not long remain under suspicion, and could not be convicted. I knew no money would be found on her person, and at the worst I thought a verdict of manslaughter in self-defence would be passed, and she would in the end go free. For her subsequent career I meant to answer myself, so that not only should she not suffer for my deed, but actually be the gainer."

The man was so glib, that he actually puzzled the authorities for some time. No one for a moment believed in the motive he ascribed to himself, but it was a little difficult to find the real one. In the event, however, the whole mystery was cleared up by the arrival of the writer of the anonymous letter from Siberia, induced to throw off his anonymity by a carefully-worded advertisement in Siberian newspapers. As soon as Gorbunov was brought face to face with this man he turned deadly white, and from that moment, to the not distant day of his death refused to say a word in explanation of his conduct. The immediate recognition of Gorbunov by the man from Siberia as the notorious Milutin, the last member of the "White Eagle" left untraced, put the matter beyond all doubt, and the execution of the murderer Gorbunov and counter-revolutionary Milutin put an end for ever to the mystery of the Pavlov case, and wound up for ever the affairs of the "White Eagle".

THE TRUTH ABOUT A
DETECTIVE STORY

NOT VERY MANY writers know exactly what it was that made them write a particular story at a particular time in a particular form. *I* do.

I had been wanting to write *a* book for several years, ever since I had had two novels out in England in my early twenties, but couldn't get started on a third. Then I married and had two children and went to live in Moscow after the 1917 Revolution, and still I wanted to write another book and still I couldn't. I loved my husband and I loved my children, but I was insatiable. I wanted to write a book. My husband was out all day and my children were in kindergarten, so there would have been plenty of time, but all I could get out of myself were a few articles for the Woman's Page of the *Manchester Guardian*; once or twice I made the back page with a story. I had an article about E. M. Forster accepted in some Soviet monthly, one short story, called "Street-car Fantasy", in the Moscow evening newspaper and another called "She Didn't Understand", in the weekly *Ogonyok*, in the issue that had a photograph of the poet Yessenin in his open coffin on the same page, but I didn't even begin to try and write a novel. And that was what I wanted to do. The longer I went on not writing a novel the more melancholy I became.

Reading was the next thing I most wanted to do. First of all I read all the Russian classics I had only read in English before, and then I discovered the second-hand bookshops, the *bookinisti* of Moscow, and read a lot of old English books I had never read in England and some I had read and forgotten and was very glad to see again, such as *Hereward the Wake*, and *Trilby* and *Sartor Resantus*, and *Lob-Lie-by-the-Fire* for the children. One day the Commandant of the house we were living in gave me the key of the library and I found a whole wall of Tauchnitz editions of once-popular English novels and read through batteries of re-bound Trollopes, Disraelis and Mrs. Gaskells and a lot of other books I would probably never have read if I had stayed in England. I enjoyed them but they didn't seem to be a help to writing: they all seemed to have been written for good and all. They gave me an idea for an article in the *Manchester Guardian*, "A Good Bold Baron", meaning Baron Tauchnitz. When I say Tauchnitz now, people look blank, which astonished me at first because the Tauchnitz editions of English books continued up to our own times, but then I realised most English people had never seen one because they were forbidden for copyright reasons to be brought into England and could only be read in foreign countries. Whenever Tolstoi went abroad he came back with *The Lady in White* or *Lady Audley's Secret*, or *Barchester Towers* and read them aloud to his family in the evenings, translating as he read. That's why I called my article "A Good Bold Baron", because Tauchnitz gave people in foreign countries a chance to read English books in the original.

When we first went to Russia we had two large rooms in a rambling mansion on the embankment then called Sofiskaya Naberezhnaya. Our windows were exactly opposite the Kremlin Palace on the other side of the river. The Palace and the rambling mansion across the river are still there, but one is now the Soviet Hall of Congress and the other houses the British Embassy. Our rooms were at one end of a long hall on the first floor, and rooms at the other end were sometimes allotted to distinguished foreigners. I never knew who they were and although I occasionally met one of them on the stairs leading to the front hall there was never any sign of greeting on either side. We might have been ghosts.

But one morning, a very short time after Lenin's death, my husband told me that a man who had just come to stay in the house ought to be of interest to me. This was a certain Professor Vogt who had founded a Brain (dead brain) Institute somewhere near Berlin and had been invited to help the foundation of a Moscow Brain Institute, first and foremost to dissect and investigate the brain of Lenin. This was not what my husband thought might interest me, he knew I had not the slightest interest in anatomy or scientific Institutes, but he had heard that Professor Vogt was a well-known hypnotist. I knew nothing about hypnotism but Svengali, and once I had seen a demonstration in a London music hall; I thought hypnotism was just another form of charlatanism, or at least could be of use only to the feeble-minded. "I think you have to be a very special person to get anything out of hypnotism," I said scornfully. "Well, I don't know who isn't a very special sort of person if you aren't," said my husband. I knew he was being neither complimentary nor denigratory—merely indulgently ironical—so his remark neither elated nor discouraged me. It was just one of those little marital crossings of swords that does nobody any harm. But I was secretly more interested than I showed. There might be something in hypnotism. It might be fun. Perhaps the professor might be able to hypnotise me into writing again. So when I passed him on the stairs the next day I thought he looked at me rather kindly. I soon discovered that he had his wife with him, and was vaguely disappointed. She was a tall austere-looking lady who wore her hair in a bun at the nape of her neck and had a rather school-teachery looking leather belt fastened with a silver buckle. But she looked kind, too, and we smiled at one another in the down-stairs hall when we chanced to meet. One day we happened to go out of the heavy front door at the same time and I greeted them in English. She spoke it fairly well, but the professor's speech was stiff and stilted. It appeared that we were going in the same direction, towards the bridge leading to the Red Square. I did not take long to ask him if it was true that he was a hypnotist. He asked me who had told me he was and when I said it had been my husband he smiled and said: "He is a great man. He knows all things, is it not so?", which I took to be an answer. He was a hypnotist. I then asked him what he thought of psycho-analysis. His wife did not put in a word, only went on looking benevolent. "And you, Gnädige Frau, what is your opinion?" I submitted modestly that my opinion could not be of any interest, only I had once been partly psycho-analysed to make me go on writing, but it had not helped me. I gathered that the professor was not surprised. He did not believe that psycho-analysis could make a person do anything. "But could hypnosis?" I asked. The professor knew of people hypnotism had helped to write a book. My heart leaped up but as he made no proposal to hypnotise me then and there in the middle of the bridge, I was too shy to ask him to do so.

Two days later I met the profesor in the hall at the foot of the enormous brown bear which had held out a brass dish for visiting cards in the old days, only somebody had stolen it, the commandant said, and now it only held out its thick paws as if it was waiting for somebody to come and be hugged. It was the professor who spoke first. He told me that the German ambassador only the night before had said to him that I spoke German beautifully, in which case he would be glad to try and help me to write a book. And I, I said, would be glad to be helped.

That very afternoon I stretched myself obediently on the sofa in the professor's sitting-room and tried to keep my eyes fixed on the brass knob of a candelabra hanging above the marble mantelpiece. I listened respectfully to his mild injunctions to relax, to keep my eyes open as long as I could (which wasn't very long; they closed of themselves), to mild assurances that there was nothing to prevent me writing a book, that I certainly would write a book, that I had nothing to fear, nothing to reproach myself with, in effect that everything was simply splendid. I listened with docile hope, but I had expected to be compelled to perform strange deeds, as I had seen at the music-hall demonstration. Above all, I had expected to fall into a deep black velvet sleep. When the professor intimated that this was enough for today I exclaimed: "But I never lost consciousness for a moment!" He explained in German that I strained hard to understand that that was not necessary, that he could easily have put me to sleep if he had wanted to, that all would be well and I would have a good night's sleep and must come to him the next day at the same time. I did not believe him, I thought he would have liked to put me to sleep but hadn't been able to. But I was happy that somebody wanted to help me. Wanting to help a person is in itself help, I thought.

I went to see the professor every day, and told him all my troubles (everyone has troubles). I always left his room feeling happier though I never stopped yearning to fall into deep unconsciousness (I don't to this day know why). Twice he was suddenly called away to the Kremlin, a car would be waiting at the porch for him. He told me to wait a moment and went for his wife to continue the session. Each time she sat down on a chair beside me (the professor usually sat at his desk or got up and moved about the room) and to my astonishment each time I fell into that deep abyss of sleep I had been so craving for. She had to wake me with a slight blow on the cheek and said: "Now go to bed and continue the sleep." I did, and awoke next morning more cheerfully than I could ever remember waking up in the morning before. I told my professor about this. "She sent me fast asleep," I said. "Ah, yes, I taught her how to. It is all she can do." "But why don't you?" I asked. "It is not what is required," he said gravely. And this time I believed him. I remembered the music-hall demonstration.

The day before they were to go home my dear professor said to me (I had become very fond of him in these few weeks and valued his concentrated goodwill towards myself): "You will sit down at your husband's writing-table as soon as he leaves every morning and write a book." "But what makes you so sure I ought to? You've never read anything I've written, what makes you believe I'm really a writer?" "Ihre ganze Wegen." I knew the meaning of his words; he meant "Everything about you", but I have never been able to find an adequate translation of them, they seemed so beautiful to me. The next morning he was gone before I was up, and as soon as my husband left for work I sat down at his writing-table and began to write a book, and it turned out a detective story because I had just read one for the first time since I shivered over Sherlock Holmes at boarding school.

IVY LITVINOV
October 1972